"I've always known you were off limits—

and even so I'm breaking all the rules."

Brittany tipped her head back and looked at Ethan. "What rules?"

"I'm talking about your age. You're so very young."

Her eyes widened. "You don't like young women?"

"You're fourteen years younger than me, Brittany. Have you ever made love with a man?"

For a moment she just looked at him, then she buried her face in his shoulder. "No. I've never before met one I wanted to be...um...*with* in that way."

Pride and regret warred within him. He brushed the hair away from her cheek. "I'm flattered that you think I might be that man," he murmured into her ear. "I wish I were, but I'm afraid I'm not."

Dear Reader,

From the enchantment of first loves to the wonder of second chances, Silhouette Romance demonstrates the power of genuine emotion. This month we continue our yearlong twentieth anniversary celebration with another stellar lineup, including the return of beloved author Dixie Browning with *Cinderella's Midnight Kiss*.

Next, Raye Morgan delivers a charming marriage-of-convenience story about a secretary who is *Promoted—To Wife!* And Silhouette Romance begins a new theme-based promotion, AN OLDER MAN, which highlights stories featuring sophisticated older men who meet their matches in younger, inexperienced women. Our premiere title is *Professor and the Nanny* by reader favorite Phyllis Halldorson.

Bestselling author Judy Christenberry unveils her new miniseries, THE CIRCLE K SISTERS, in *Never Let You Go*. When a millionaire businessman wins an executive assistant at an auction, he discovers that he wants her to be *Contractually His*...forever. Don't miss this conclusion of Myrna Mackenzie's THE WEDDING AUCTION series. And in Karen Rose Smith's *Just the Husband She Chose*, a powerful attorney is reunited in a marriage meant to satisfy a will.

In coming months, look for new miniseries by some of your favorite authors. It's an exciting year for Silhouette Books, and we invite you to join the celebration!

Happy reading!

Mary-Theresa Hussey

Mary-Theresa Hussey
Senior Editor

Please address questions and book requests to:
Silhouette Reader Service
U.S.: 3010 Walden Ave., P.O. Box 1325, Buffalo, NY 14269
Canadian: P.O. Box 609, Fort Erie, Ont. L2A 5X3

PROFESSOR AND THE NANNY

Phyllis Halldorson

Silhouette
ROMANCE™
Published by Silhouette Books
America's Publisher of Contemporary Romance

For my Friday critique group, those generous and talented writers whose support has been invaluable over the years. Many thanks and much love.

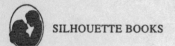

SILHOUETTE BOOKS

ISBN 0-373-19452-8

PROFESSOR AND THE NANNY

Copyright © 2000 by Phyllis Halldorson

All rights reserved. Except for use in any review, the reproduction or utilization of this work in whole or in part in any form by any electronic, mechanical or other means, now known or hereafter invented, including xerography, photocopying and recording, or in any information storage or retrieval system, is forbidden without the written permission of the editorial office, Silhouette Books, 300 East 42nd Street, New York, NY 10017 U.S.A.

All characters in this book have no existence outside the imagination of the author and have no relation whatsoever to anyone bearing the same name or names. They are not even distantly inspired by any individual known or unknown to the author, and all incidents are pure invention.

This edition published by arrangement with Harlequin Books S.A.

® and TM are trademarks of Harlequin Books S.A., used under license. Trademarks indicated with ® are registered in the United States Patent and Trademark Office, the Canadian Trade Marks Office and in other countries.

Visit Silhouette at www.eHarlequin.com

Printed in U.S.A.

Books by Phyllis Halldorson

PHYLLIS HALLDORSON

met her real-life Prince Charming at the age of sixteen. She married him a year later, and they settled down to raise a family. A compulsive reader, Phyllis dreamed of someday finding the time to write stories of her own. That time came when her two youngest children reached adolescence. When she was introduced to romance novels, she knew she had found her long-delayed vocation. After all, how could she write anything else after living all those years with her very own Silhouette hero?

IT'S OUR 20th ANNIVERSARY!
We'll be celebrating all year,
Continuing with these fabulous titles,
On sale in June 2000.

Romance

#1450 Cinderella's Midnight
Kiss
Dixie Browning

#1451 Promoted–To Wife!
Raye Morgan

AN OLDER MAN
#1452 Professor and the
Nanny
Phyllis Halldorson

The Circle K Sisters
#1453 Never Let You Go
Judy Christenberry

The WEDDING AUCTION
#1454 Contractually His
Myrna Mackenzie

#1455 Just the Husband She
Chose
Karen Rose Smith

Desire

MAN OF THE MONTH
#1297 Tough To Tame
Jackie Merritt

#1298 The Rancher and
the Nanny
Caroline Cross

MATCHED IN MONTANA
#1299 The Cowboy Meets
His Match
Meagan McKinney

#1300 Cheyenne Dad
Sheri WhiteFeather

the TOP TOY Bank
#1301 The Baby Gift
Susan Crosby

#1302 The Determined Groom
Kate Little

Intimate Moments

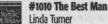

#1009 The Wildes of
Wyoming–Ace
Ruth Langan

#1010 The Best Man
Linda Turner

#1011 Beautiful Stranger
Ruth Wind

#1012 Her Secret Guardian
Sally Tyler Hayes

#1013 Undercover with the
Enemy
Christine Michels

#1014 The Lawman's Last
Stand
Vickie Taylor

Special Edition

#1327 The Baby Quilt
Christine Flynn

#1328 Irish Rebel
Nora Roberts

#1329 To a MacAllister
Born
Joan Elliott Pickart

#1330 A Man Apart
Ginna Gray

#1331 The Sheik's Secret
Bride
Susan Mallery

#1332 The Price of Honor
Janis Reams Hudson

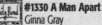

Chapter One

Brittany Baldwin's stomach churned as she pulled over to the curb and parked in front of the white colonial-style house with two-story-high pillars that supported the overhang above the porch.

It was a lovely upper-middle-class home in a historic neighborhood of Lexington, and the man she was supposed to meet here was a professor of literature at the University of Kentucky, but was she ready for this? Her first interview for her first nursing job. She'd expected to have three more years of college before actually going to work, but then...

She shook her head as if the sharp movement could drive away the searing memories that still haunted her, then got out of the car and walked briskly up to the door. The bell chimed melodiously when pushed and the door was opened by a good-looking man of medium height with light brown hair and eyes to match behind silver-framed glasses.

For a moment they just stood there looking at each other, each waiting for the other to speak.

Finally he broke the silence. "Yes?"

It was put in the form of a question, but why? Surely he was expecting her.

"I...I'm Brittany Baldwin," she stammered, "the medical assistant Professor Thorpe requested."

He blinked. "*You're* the nurse I asked for?"

"Nursing *assistant*," she corrected him, "and yes, if you're Professor Ethan Thorpe, I was told to meet you here at—" she paused and looked at her watch "—four o'clock."

He was still frowning at her. "Is there a problem?" she asked.

"You could say that, yes," he growled. "I am Ethan Thorpe, but you'd better come in while we discuss it."

She wondered what there was to discuss as he stood aside so she could step into the large tiled foyer that housed a wide staircase in the center and displayed a magnificent crystal chandelier suspended from the soaring ceiling.

Brittany was impressed, but before she could comment the man had taken her arm and was ushering her into the area to the right. His hand cupping her elbow was firm but warm and smooth, and she involuntarily leaned into it, seeking its security.

This room was a parlor furnished with beautiful antique furniture, and he led her to the settee and motioned for her to sit down. She did, reluctantly relinquishing his supporting touch, and he took a high-backed wing chair several feet away.

"Now, Ms....Baldwin did you say your name is?"

"Brittany," she murmured, and he continued. "I'm afraid there's been a misunderstanding. I asked for a mature, well-trained and experienced woman capable of taking care of my father, who is diabetic and has difficulty with his short-term memory."

Brittany still didn't understand the problem. "I admit I'm not very experienced, but I'm well trained in nursing care as I'm sure the agency told you. I can administer his shots, oversee his diet and watch him so he doesn't wander off—"

"How old are you?" Ethan interjected.

"I'm...uh...I'm twenty-one, but I'm well aware of the responsibility involved in caring for my patients," she hastily assured him. "I was studying to be a registered nurse but..."

She bit back her ill-advised words and hoped he hadn't caught them. She really didn't want to get into that subject right now. It was still too painful to discuss with strangers, and besides, it had nothing to do with her nursing skills. She'd learned those at the vocational school after—

Unfortunately his hearing was keen and so was his curiosity. "Brittany? You were saying...?"

"Oh, nothing," she replied, groping for a way out. "It really doesn't apply to this situation."

He leaned back in his chair and captured her gaze. The lenses of his glasses weren't very thick, and she could see the flecks of gold in his brown pupils behind them. The metal frames were circular and softened the wideness of his cheekbones and the squareness of his jaw. He looked to be in his early or mid-thirties, and was a very handsome man in a quiet sort of way.

"Why don't you let me be the judge of that?" he suggested softly but with a hint of determination that would not be denied.

Oh well, this was, after all, an interview for a job. He had a right to ask questions, and if she wanted the position she'd better answer them. She just hoped she could get through it without breaking down!

She twined her hands in her lap and leaned forward as she began. "Last year I completed my first year at the university. I was working for a degree in nursing, but then in August my..."

Her voice shook and she swallowed. "...my parents were killed in a boating accident."

He sat bolt upright in his chair. "Oh, look, I'm sorry. I had no idea. I didn't mean to put you through this...."

She held up her hand. "No, please, it's something I have to learn to live with."

With her fingertips she dabbed at the unwelcome tears that had formed in her eyes. "When the estate was settled I learned they had been living beyond their means for years and were on the verge of bankruptcy. All I managed to salvage was Mom's car, which by some miracle was paid for, and enough money to enroll in the medical assistant's program at the career vocational school here in town."

She took a deep breath. "It was a ten-month course and I graduated last week. This is my first job interview."

"But surely you have relatives," he muttered.

She shook her head. "Not unless you count two second cousins living in California whom I haven't seen in almost ten years. I have no brothers or sisters, aunts or uncles."

"Well I have to admit you come highly recommended by your school," he said, "but you're so *young*. And so *fragile*."

Brittany couldn't help it, she laughed. "There's not much I can do about the 'young' part, but 'fragile'? Professor Thorpe, I'm five feet six inches tall and weigh one-hundred-thirty pounds. I've also had strength training and my body is very well toned."

Ethan grinned. "Don't underestimate my dad. He's over six feet tall, slimmer now than he used to be, but still tips the scales at close to two hundred pounds, and makes up in just plain wiliness for what he may have lost in muscle power."

The cool reserve between the two of them had been broken, and they sat back and relaxed. "Tell me a little about your father," Brittany said. "I understand he's retired now, but what did he do for a living? How many children does he have? What about your mother? That type of thing."

She knew she was assuming a lot here, asking questions like that before she'd even been hired, but she really wanted this job and she wasn't going to make it easy for the professor to send her away if his only objection to her was her age.

"You want to know what my dad used to do for a living?" Ethan inquired. "He spent forty years as a heavy-equipment repairer. He's got muscles you never heard of, and most of them are still fully operational even though he doesn't exercise much anymore. You'd have a time controlling him if he didn't want to be controlled. Fortunately, he's even-tempered and he'd die before he'd ever touch a woman in anger."

"Then we don't have to worry about my strength or lack of it, do we," she said sweetly with a touch of sarcasm.

"But it's not your well being I'm worried about," Ethan replied. "He sometimes loses his balance and falls. Are you strong enough to help him get up and patient enough to give him constant attention? He tends to get confused and wanders away if not supervised."

"It's almost impossible for any one person to lift a patient who can't help himself," she told him, "but I can certainly dial 911 if I need help. I'm prepared to do whatever is necessary to keep him safe and well as long as he's under my supervision. How old is he?"

"He's seventy-two and in good health as long as he keeps his diabetes under control, but because of his short-term memory problems he can't always remember to give himself his insulin shots. When that happens he goes downhill fast, but I'm sure you know about that."

Brittany knew he was testing her and responded appropriately. "Yes, I do. His blood-sugar count goes up dangerously high and he feels woozy. That's when he's apt to get confused and fall."

Ethan nodded his agreement. "Right. That's the most important reason we need a medical assistant as a caregiver."

"I'm very good at making sure my patients get their meds," she assured him. "What about your mother? Does she live here, too?"

He shook his head. "My mother died of a sudden heart attack when my twin brother and I were in high school. Peter and I were their only children, and Dad never married again so there's no second family.''

"And your wife?'' she asked hesitantly. ''You do have a wife, don't you?''

He shook his head. ''Not anymore,'' he said crisply. ''My wife and I were divorced two years ago. We have an eighteen-month-old son, but he won't be a problem for you. He lives in Pleasant Hill with his mother. I have him every other weekend.''

Brittany was startled by his disclosure. So far she hadn't seen any sign of a woman in residence, but she'd assumed there was one. Why would any woman give up on a man with all Ethan had going for him? What had happened?

Well, that was obviously none of her business and it was time to change the subject.

"So you have a twin brother,'' she said. ''That must have been fun when you were growing up.''

He smiled. ''No, we're fraternal twins, not identical. Pete is six two, losing his hair and has blue eyes. We don't even look like brothers.''

Brittany's gaze shifted up to Ethan's luxuriant crop of brown-colored hair, and her fingers tingled to run through it. No chance of him going bald anytime soon. ''How odd,'' she commented. ''Does he live in the area?''

"No, he and his wife are lawyers and are partners in separate law firms in New Orleans, so you'd be on your own with Dad from eight in the morning until midafternoon at the earliest. Do you think you could handle that?''

"I'm sure of it,'' she said with a tad more confidence than she felt. ''Also, the agency I work through has backup help always available. I can call them at any time should a problem arise.''

"Well, I don't know,'' he waffled. ''I need someone who understands the situation and can deal with it. My first choice was for a male medical assistant, but the agency didn't have any available.''

He thought for a minute, then spoke. "Look, why don't I introduce you to Dad and see how it goes? He's in the family room watching a baseball game on television.''

"I think that's a great idea,'' Brittany said, relieved that he was at least going to give her a chance, let her meet the patient and see how they got along.

"Fine, then come on. It's down the hall.''

Again he took her arm. She wasn't sure it was necessary as a form of politeness, but she was glad he did. She liked the closeness it induced in her.

They walked down the hall to the right of the staircase and past a closed door until they came to a big open room across the back of the house.

It was totally unlike the parlor, or the dining room she'd glimpsed across the foyer. They were furnished in eighteenth-century decor, stately but cool and formal. This one, however, was strictly twentieth century with comfortable modern furniture, massive sliding glass doors and windows with a view that seemed to bring the colorful, well-tended gardens inside. A big-screen television set was tuned to a baseball game in progress.

The furniture divided the rectangular room into two separate areas. The television was the focal point to the left of the wide entryway, and the right side featured a marble fireplace with a long cream-colored sofa facing it from the middle of the room. There were numerous thickly upholstered lounge chairs in shades of brown, rust and beige positioned around both sides, and lamps strategically placed for reading.

An older man sat in one of the chairs with his back to them, avidly watching the screen, and didn't hear them approach until Ethan spoke. "Dad, would you turn the sound down? We have a visitor.''

The man looked around, startled, and immediately turned

off the set with the remote, then struggled to his feet. "Sorry, I didn't hear you coming," he said pleasantly.

"Please don't apologize," Brittany said, and held out her hand. "I'm Brittany Baldwin."

She didn't know just what she'd expected, but this wasn't it. Nate Thorpe was tall and slender, somewhat loosely put together, like a dancer, except she could tell from the way he swayed ever so slightly when he first stood that he had a problem with his balance.

He took her hand. His grip was firm and his eyes brown like his son's. In fact, he and Ethan looked quite a bit alike, except Nate's hair had turned iron-gray and he wore a mustache. He also wore glasses, but his were thicker than his son's and had tortoiseshell rims.

His eyes sparkled as his gaze traveled over her and he smiled. "My short-term memory might not be what it used to be, but I know I'd remember you if we'd ever met before."

Good, Brittany thought. He was playful, which meant he probably wasn't depressed.

"Brittany is here to interview for the position of medical assistant," Ethan told him. "Remember? I told you about it this morning."

"Of course I remember," Nate snapped. "I may be old but I'm not senile yet."

Brittany winced and she saw Ethan flush. "Dad, I wasn't implying that you are—"

He paused, obviously unsure of how to handle the situation.

She wasn't, either, but she stepped in, anyway. She and Nate were still holding hands after shaking them, and she squeezed his. "We all forget things at times," she said lightly. "I have to write everything down if I don't want to forget it, and this college professor son of yours didn't even know who I was when I showed up on your doorstep right on time for this appointment. One he had set up. Everyone's got problems, sir."

Nate tightened his grip on her hand, then let her go. "Hire her, son, before she gets away. If I gotta be sick, I want her for a nurse."

Ethan knew when he'd been outclassed, outwitted and out-maneuvered. What he couldn't figure out was how it had happened! One minute he'd had everything under control and the next his own father and the nurse he hadn't even hired yet had wrested it from him and were dictating their own terms.

Well, that was okay. He wanted Nate to make his own decisions for as long as he was able to. If Nate wanted a nurse who was young and easy to look at as well as well trained, then Ethan would at least give Ms. Baldwin a try. After all, he could always let her go if she proved inadequate.

"All right, Dad," he said agreeably. "If Brittany and I can come to terms, she's all yours. Now, you turn your game back on and we'll go in the library and work things out."

Nate grinned. "Glad to have you on board, missy," he said, and sat back down.

Ethan involuntarily reached out to take Brittany's arm again, but then thought better of it. There was no professional reason for him to touch her, and he liked the prickles that traveled up and down his own hand and arm when he did so altogether too much.

He hadn't counted on hiring such an attractive nurse. Attractive! She was downright beautiful. Her rich, dark brown hair was parted in the middle and hung free to her shoulders with bangs across her forehead. He ached to run his fingers through it and feel its softness. Her eyes were grass-green and looked at him with wide speculation that made his blood rush to his head. *Sexy* wasn't nearly a strong enough word to describe the way she walked and talked.

But she was also little more than a child. Twenty-one years old. A lot of his students were older than that. Hell, he'd already been fourteen when she was born!

Enough of that, he thought as he preceded her to the closed door they'd passed earlier and opened it into the library. This was his favorite room, smaller than the others with a brick fireplace, bookshelf-lined walls, a leather sofa, a large mahogany desk and a couple of desk chairs. He could relax in here, renew his energy and prepare his lessons and lectures for upcoming classes.

He found it a good place to try to clear his mind of the unsettling problems and troubling speculations his father's illnesses had brought with them. He invited Brittany to sit down, then took the chair behind the desk.

"You have a beautiful home," she said as she looked around. "How I envy you these books. Have you read all of them?"

"Most of them," he admitted. "The house and antique furnishings were a legacy from my mother. She was a true Southern lady. Impeccable manners and charm were born and bred into her from generations going back to before the Civil War. She inherited the house from her father and in turn passed it on to Dad when she died."

He leaned forward and put his arms on the desk. "It's awfully big for just the two of us, and it's getting more and more expensive to keep up, but we could never sell it."

"Of course you couldn't. You and your brother will want to pass it on to your children." There was sympathy mixed with understanding in her tone.

Much as he appreciated her empathy, she wasn't here to discuss his problems and he pulled his attention back to the subject at hand. "Do you really want this job, Brittany?"

She opened her mouth to speak, but he held up his hand to stop her. "Think carefully before you answer. Given proper attention to his diabetes Nate could live for another twenty years."

Again she opened her mouth and once more he silenced

her. "No, hear me out. I certainly don't expect you to spend the next twenty years of your life taking care of us—"

He heard himself say "us" and snapped his mouth shut. That wasn't what he'd meant! She wouldn't be hired to look after *him*. Just his father!

He felt the flush that colored his face but decided to ignore it and go on. "That is, I realize you would eventually want to go back to school to get your bachelor of science degree in nursing, or get married and move away, whatever, but I don't want Nate subjected to a new caretaker every few months. He gets confused enough without adding that to the indignities he has to endure."

Too late he saw the irritation that contorted her face as she stood and braced her arms with her hands flat on the desk.

"What right do you have to assume that nursing is just a hobby with me?" she asked angrily as he leaned back. "One I can work at when I want to, and walk away from when I don't?"

He tried to answer but she hurried on. "Is it because I'm young? Well, don't judge me by the way you may have acted when you were twenty-one. I take my work seriously, and if this is your way of asking if there's a man in my life the answer is no, there isn't. As for going back to the university, it will be years before I can afford to do that. I'm still trying to pay off Mom's and Dad's bills."

Ethan was taken aback, but he also jumped up and glared at her across the desk. "Now, just a minute. I wasn't implying you aren't good at your job, I just want some assurance that you won't get bored after a few months and leave Nate for something more exciting—"

"Do you call diabetes and forgetfulness boring?" she asked.

"No, of course not," he said more softly. "I know firsthand

what a big job it is, but doing the same thing day after day for a sick old man is bound to get monotonous.''

"I don't think of Nate as a 'sick old man.''" Her tone had lowered, too. "I think of him as a man who needs the help that I can provide, and every stride we make forward will be exciting.''

Ethan sank back down in his chair and wasn't surprised to see his hands shaking. "Please, sit down. I don't usually get this emotional. It's probably because I haven't had to face the gravity of dad's illness until now. He's had the diabetes for several years but knew how to take care of himself so there was no problem.

"It was about a year ago that he started having difficulty with his blood sugar, and that's when we discovered he hadn't been getting his shots regularly. After a few other tests, the doctor told us Nate had developed the early stages of senility, which often shows up in diabetics, and that was causing him to forget to give himself the injections.''

He ran his hands over his face. This was harder than he'd expected. He suspected he hadn't really faced his father's illness before. It was so much easier to hide from it, pretend it was a temporary inconvenience that would eventually go away.

"That's when I sold my house and moved in here with him so I could monitor him, remind him to take his shots and fix his meals," he continued, "but there were still the dietary restrictions and the blood tests. Now he's started wandering off and getting lost. So far I've managed to find him without much trouble, but he needs full-time care and I can't give it to him and still keep my day job, which we need to live on.''

He looked at Brittany and she saw the anguish in his eyes. "I didn't mean to insult you or imply that you wouldn't take proper care of him, but I have to be sure the person I hire is reliable, and you're so young and so beautiful. I can't believe you'd be content to put up with the irritation a patient in Nate's condition can cause.''

Her heart melted at the torment in his voice, and without thinking she got up and walked around the desk to stand beside his chair. "Ethan, I'm well qualified to watch over your father and see to it that he gets his medication.''

She put her hand gently on his slumped shoulder. He was only wearing a lightweight shirt, and she could feel the warmth of his bare skin beneath it. "I think he and I would get along really well together. I like him, and he seems to like me.''

She started to lift her hand away, belatedly aware she was taking a liberty she shouldn't be, but he reached across his chest and held it where it was. She felt his muscles twitch beneath her palm.

"What's not to like?" he said hoarsely. "When can you start?''

Chapter Two

Brittany shivered as she stood in front of the open door of the closet in her one-room apartment, clad only in a set of the expensive pastel lingerie her mother had bought her. Not that she was cold. She wasn't. She was having an attack of nerves.

She'd been so confident of her ability as a medical assistant when under the watchful eye of her instructors, but from today on she'd be alone with her patient, with no one to tell her what to do if something unexpected should happen.

Her gaze traveled over the contents of the closet. What would the Thorpes want her to wear? She hadn't thought to ask them. Some patients still expected nurses to wear white starched uniforms, but those had gone out of style years ago. In the hospital she wore a white lab coat over green scrubs, but in training for home visits she'd usually donned jeans and a T-shirt under the lab coat. Cleaning up after patients at home could get pretty messy at times.

She finally decided on a beige pantsuit that looked professional and was machine-washable, a necessity in her occupation. Since Nate was more in need of supervision than medical attention, she'd been designated his caregiver, so she didn't think he or Ethan would mind if she dressed casually in her own clothes.

Grabbing two freshly laundered lab coats and her medical kit, she hurried out the door and locked it behind her.

Ethan told himself he wasn't pacing the floor and that he was just wandering around the house while he waited for his dad's nurse to arrive. However, it felt like pacing to him. A glance at his watch told him Brittany wasn't late, rather he was early. It was only eight o'clock, and even with commuting time he didn't have to leave the house until eight-thirty, but he wanted to go over some things with her before he left.

The chime of the bell a few minutes later sent him striding quickly to the door. He opened it and caught his breath. She was even more lovely than he'd remembered. The tan pantsuit she was wearing was strictly tailored, even masculine in its lines, but there was nothing androgynous in the way she filled it out. Her full breasts thrust gently against the material of the blouse, and the curve of her hips under the slacks was definitely not mannish.

It was a good thing they would meet for only a few minutes each day coming and going. He'd never be able to resist the temptation she was stirring in him if it lasted much longer!

"Professor? Is something the matter?" Her voice broke into his musing, and he realized he'd been standing there staring at her like a starstruck teenager.

He blinked and shook his head. "No, please, come in."

He moved aside to let her pass him, and got a whiff of the aroma of spring flowers. Delicate and pleasing.

"Where's your dad?" she asked as she deposited her purse and her medical kit on the table in the foyer.

"He's not up yet," Ethan said. "Lately I've been having to wake him to give him his shot and his breakfast before I leave to go to the university, but that interrupts his rest. Now that you'll be coming every morning he can sleep a little longer."

She smiled. "Fine. I'll be happy to take over."

"How about a cup of coffee?" he asked, glancing at his watch even though he knew exactly what time it was. He hoped the gesture would make her think it was a spur-of-the-moment invitation rather than the eagerly thought-out proposal it really was. "I don't have to leave for a few minutes yet."

"I'd like that," Brittany said softly, and walked with him through the kitchen on the left side of the staircase to the small room they called the breakfast room. Ethan had pointed it out to her when he took her on a tour of the house the day he hired her. The sun streaming through the sheer curtains that covered the large windows flooded the area with light and bathed it in an aura of cheerfulness.

There was a round table and four chairs in the middle of the room, and two other chairs in the corners. A chest-high breakfast bar separated the two rooms, and potted tropical plants added shafts of color.

The electric coffeemaker was set up on the bar counter, and Ethan stopped to pour coffee into the mugs while Brittany pulled out a chair and sat down.

"Cream and sugar?" he asked.

"Black," she told him, and he brought the two cups to the table and sat down beside her.

"I've left a list of phone numbers you can call for help if anything should go wrong," he told her. "Mine at the university is at the top, of course, but there's also Dad's doctor, the next-door neighbors on either side of us and, as a last resort, my brother and his wife in New Orleans."

"Thank you, I'm glad to have those," she said. "I'm also interested in knowing what his limitations are aside from his occasional confusion. Can I take him out for rides or walks, or maybe a shopping trip?"

"Oh, sure, he loves to get out," Ethan assured her. "That's

one of the biggest problems I've had with him lately. When he's here alone he goes out and then can't find his way back home."

A voice from behind Brittany startled them both. It was Nate's. "Ethan, you got any idea what time it is? Why didn't you wake me up? You're gonna be late...."

Brittany turned in her chair to look at him standing there in his rumpled pajamas, hair tousled, and an emerging twenty-four-hour beard.

He saw her at the same time and his eyes opened wide with shock. "Damn," he bellowed, "why didn't you tell me we had company?"

Nate crossed his arms over his chest and bent at the waist in an attempt to cover himself.

"She isn't company, Dad, this is the woman I hired for you—"

"You got me a woman!" he sputtered in disbelieving amazement. "Look, son, I may be gettin' older but I can still find my own girlfriends."

Brittany couldn't help it, she put her head back and laughed gleefully. Not that the fact Nate didn't remember her was funny, but the looks on both his and Ethan's faces were hilarious.

"No!" Ethan said, frustration mixed with compassion in his tone. "This is Brittany. She's going to be your nurse-companion?"

She saw the confusion in Nate's expression, but it was clear that he wasn't going to give in to it.

"Well, my memory's not so good," he admitted, "but you got to admit my taste is impeccable." He winked at her and put out his hand. "Welcome, young lady. Please pardon my get-up, but it's not often I find a beautiful woman at my breakfast table."

She put her hand in his and chuckled. "That's hard to believe and, please, call me Brittany."

He squeezed her hand and released it. "That's a pretty name. Almost as pretty as the girl who bears it."

Brittany tampered down the ire she always felt when called a 'girl.' After all, this man could be forgiven. He was of another generation when that title was both common and acceptable. "Thank you, Mr. Thorpe, but I'm no longer a 'girl.' I'm twenty-one years old. Old enough to drink hard liquor and vote."

She caught the impish glee in his eyes even before he spoke. "Not at the same time, I hope."

They both chuckled, and Ethan joined in as he pushed his chair back from the table and stood. "Now that we all have our identities straightened out, I've got to leave."

Brittany stood up, too, and both she and Nate walked to the door with Ethan. When they got there he turned to Brittany. "The list of phone numbers I told you about is in the library on my desk. Don't hesitate to call me if you need anything."

"I won't," she said as he let himself out.

When he was gone she turned to Nate. "Do you want me to give you your blood test and injection now or would you rather wait until you've dressed and shaved?"

He grimaced. "I don't need you to do that for me. I can do it myself."

She wasn't surprised at his resistance. He'd probably be more amenable after she'd been taking care of him for a while.

"Is that the way you prefer to do it?" she asked.

"Yeah."

"All right," she said agreeably, "but you'll have to walk me through it the first time so I can make sure you're doing it right. It's just a precaution."

She knew it would be easier to get his cooperation if he thought he was doing her a favor.

"Sure. We keep all the stuff in the first-floor bath." He turned and they walked together to the large Victorian-style bathroom, complete with a free-standing claw-footed tub and a commode that flushed with a chain.

Nate opened a wooden cabinet and took out the paraphernalia he needed, then stuck the end of his finger and pricked out a little blood with a sterilized needle to test on the glucose monitor. Everything there was okay so he filled the syringe and gave himself the injection in the stomach.

He'd been right. He was very good at this. If only he could remember to do it as often as required.

"Mr. Thorpe, can you—" she started to say, but he cut her off.

"Hold on there, missy, you don't like to be called a girl, and I'm not all that hot about bein' called an old man—"

Brittany gasped. "I never—"

"Oh, I know you're too polite to actually say it, but why do you have to keep calling me 'Mr. Thorpe'? It's so formal. My first name is Nate. Any reason why you can't call me that?"

She grinned. "None at all, Nate. Now, why don't you go upstairs and get dressed while I fix breakfast. Remember, you have to eat within half an hour after taking the shot or you're apt to get woozy. I don't want you tumbling down that magnificent staircase."

He chuckled. "I'll bet you're used to having men fall for you," he teased.

Things went very well for the next two weeks. Nate didn't forget who she was again and greeted her enthusiastically each morning when she arrived. They enjoyed each other's company and got along just fine all day, but it was a different scenario with Ethan. He left as soon as she arrived at the house, and was coolly polite when he got home.

It seemed obvious that he didn't especially like her, but why? He never complained about her work. At times during the few minutes of their comings and goings he even complimented her on how well his father was doing under her care, so why wasn't he more friendly?

If he had a girlfriend there was no evidence of it. The only family photographs in the house were one of Ethan's infant son, Danny, an adorable little tyke, which was displayed on the fireplace mantel in the family room, and one of Nate's late wife, Sybil, Ethan's mother, which Nate kept on his nightstand in his bedroom.

She wished Ethan would ask her to stay and visit sometimes. Maybe even invite her to dinner. She knew they did quite a bit of barbecuing in the evenings, but in the two weeks she'd been there they'd never mentioned having dinner guests.

Then, on the Thursday of the second week, a few minutes before Ethan was due home, the doorbell rang. Brittany, who had been rinsing dishes in the sink, grabbed a towel and headed for the foyer, but Nate beat her to the front door. He opened it and she saw his shoulders stiffen as he said, "Hannah? What are you doing here? Where's the baby?"

Brittany stopped in her tracks. Hannah? Baby? Could this be Ethan's ex-wife and their son?

Brittany stood there listening to a woman's voice coming from outside. "He's out in the car. Can you help me bring some things in?"

"Sure," Nate said, and walked out the door where Brittany could no longer see or hear them.

Curiosity got the better of her, and she put down the towel and walked over to the open doorway. There she saw a white minivan with the side door open parked at the curb in front of the house. Inside was a child strapped into a car seat and a blond, statuesque woman wearing designer jeans and T-shirt and loading Nate down with various items of baby furniture.

What was going on here? Nate shouldn't be burdened with all those heavy and ungainly items. He might stumble and fall!

Without hesitation she hurried out the door and across the

lawn to the curb to confront him. "Nate, don't try to carry all that stuff at once. Let me help you."

The sound of her voice apparently surprised the woman, who had been leaning in the van to retrieve several suitcases. She backed out and glared at Brittany.

"Who are you?" she asked gruffly.

"I'm Brittany Baldwin, Mr. Thorpe's caregiver, and you are…?" She wasn't going to let this woman intimidate her. She took her orders from Ethan and no one else.

"I'm Hannah Thorpe," she said sharply, then turned her attention again to Nate. "When did you get a caregiver, Nate?"

He shrugged. "It was after the last time you were here. She takes real good care of me."

Hannah looked Brittany up and down. "I'll bet she does." Her tone was venomous. "Takes real good care of your son, too, I should imagine. I figured it wouldn't be long before Ethan would take up with some other woman, but I expected her to be full grown."

Brittany gasped. "Now, wait just a darn minute—" she started to protest, but Hannah was already halfway up the driveway to the house with the suitcases.

Brittany and Nate followed close behind with the pieces of baby furniture.

"Why are you bringing all this stuff over here?" Nate asked as they set their burdens down in the foyer. "We've got all we need to take care of Danny for his weekend visits."

"Tell you later," she said as she turned and hurried outside again, Nate and Brittany not far behind.

They all reached the van at the same time and again Hannah spoke to Nate. "You and Florence Nightingale here can finish emptying the van and I'll get Danny."

Brittany bristled at the mockery in the other woman's tone but saw no point in pressing the issue.

Hannah climbed inside the vehicle and started unbuckling

the baby from the car seat while Brittany and Nate waited for her to finish so they could get in to retrieve the other articles.

While they stood there waiting, Ethan's car turned into the driveway and he got out. "What's going on?" he asked as Hannah backed out of the van with the toddler in her arms. "This isn't my weekend to have Danny."

"It is now," she said crisply, and held the child out to him. "Here, take him. He's heavy."

Ethan took his son and nuzzled him playfully on the neck. He was an adorable child with blond curly hair and sparkling blue eyes. "Hi, guy," Ethan said as he lifted the kicking and giggling little one over his head. "To what do I owe the unexpected pleasure of your company?"

"Da-da," the little boy burbled, and grabbed a fistful of his daddy's hair.

Ethan didn't display pictures of Danny all around his house, Brittany thought, but the look on his face when he hugged his little son left no doubt of his love and pride in the youngster.

"I'm glad to hear you consider his company a pleasure," Hannah said sourly, "because you're going to get plenty of it. I'm moving to Chicago tomorrow, so I'm afraid he's all yours."

Brittany couldn't believe what she'd heard, and apparently neither could Ethan. "You're what?" he roared.

"You heard me," she snapped, "but let's go inside so the neighbors aren't treated to an earful."

She wrestled a high chair out of the van and carried it up the driveway, followed by Ethan carrying Danny. Neither Brittany nor Nate knew what to do, but they finally grabbed some boxes and brought up the rear.

Back inside the house Ethan picked up a folded playpen and led the way down the hall to the family room. The others put down their burdens and followed. When they reached their destination Ethan put the youngster on his feet and Danny immediately took off running from table to sofa to chair, all the while squealing with delight.

"This room has been pretty much childproofed," Ethan said. "I'll let him run around for a while, but we can put him in the playpen if he starts getting into things."

Hannah slumped down on the sofa with a sigh. Even in jeans and no makeup she looked like a model. Her complexion was radiant and her short, blunt-cut hair was blond with golden highlights.

"I need a drink," she announced. "I've been going at top speed all day and still I'm nowhere near ready."

"Ready for what?" Ethan demanded. "What's this nonsense about moving to Chicago? I'm telling you right now, if you're planning to transfer up there, forget it. I'll never give my permission for you to take Danny so far away."

She shrugged. "I'm not asking you to. I can't take him with me. I've been offered one of those once-in-a-lifetime promotions, but I'll have to headquarter out of the Chicago office. Also I'll be traveling a lot, both national and international. So, I'm leaving Danny with you. You've always complained that you don't get to see enough of him."

She straightened up and looked around. "Where's my drink? Surely one of you big strong men can fix me a margarita."

"I'll do it," Nate volunteered, then looked at Brittany. "Come with me and I'll show you where the liquor cabinet is."

She already knew where the liquor was kept, but she also realized that she had no business standing around eavesdropping on the Thorpes' private conversation.

A hot flush stained her cheeks and she hurried along beside Nate on their way to the kitchen.

"I'm sorry you had to hear all that," he said gruffly. "When those two start having at it, things can get pretty heated."

"I'm the one who's sorry," Brittany corrected him. "I should have left the minute Ethan got home. It's just that everything happened so fast— Where does Ms. Thorpe work?"

"She's a big shot in a company that manufactures computer parts, and she's determined to break through the glass ceiling and make it all the way to the top. And don't apologize," Nate said. "I'm glad you stayed. Do me a favor and don't leave yet."

Brittany blinked. "But all this is really none of my business—"

"Don't be too sure," Nate said as they reached the kitchen. "Ethan's gonna need help tonight, and much as I love my frisky little grandson I can't keep up with him."

Nate retrieved the key to the liquor cabinet from its hiding place in a drawer, opened it and fixed Hannah's drink. "My sons think I don't know how infirm I am and I let 'em believe that, but I do know. I won't risk lettin' little Danny get hurt or lost because I had one of my spells of confusion when I was supposed to be watchin' him."

He finished mixing the cocktail and picked up the glass. "I'll pay you overtime, of course."

Brittany noticed that his hands were shaking and she silently but firmly took the glass from him before it spilled. This was a sign that his blood sugar was low and it was imperative that he eat something.

"Of course I'll stay if you want me to," she assured him, "but as a friend, not a nurse. There will be no talk of paying me overtime. Now, get a peach out of the fridge and eat it while I take this drink to Ms. Thorpe."

He smiled. "You're a sweet girl—uh, I mean woman. Sorry, I forgot—"

She felt a rush of affection much as she would feel for a grandfather if she still had one.

"That's all right." There was a catch in her voice. "I'll

make an exception for you. You may call me a girl anytime you want to.''

She turned and walked toward the family room.

As she got closer she heard Ethan and Hannah arguing. "There's no way I can take Danny full-time on such short notice," Ethan said angrily. "You might at least have given me a few weeks' warning.''

"I just got word of the promotion yesterday," Hannah explained testily, "and it's predicated on whether or not I can be there and take over on Monday. I agree it's unreasonable, but don't forget I didn't want a baby in the first place. If you'd used a little more restraint…''

She let the sentence trail off as Brittany felt the hot flush of embarrassment. "I worked hard to get where I am in my career today," Hannah continued, "and I don't intend to give it up. Besides, we always agreed that as soon as Danny was old enough you'd take physical custody of him.''

She glanced up and saw Brittany coming through the doorway with her cocktail. "Well, it's about time," she snapped.

Brittany clenched her jaw in an effort not to respond to the other woman's taunt. As she walked over to the couch and handed the drink to Hannah, the baby let out a wail from the front of the house. Ethan turned and strode quickly up the hall, leaving Brittany and Hannah alone. Neither spoke at first, then Hannah said, "Are you really a nurse?''

"I'm a medical assistant," Brittany explained. "I see to it that Nate gets his shots and his meals on time, and watch him to make sure he doesn't wander off.''

Hannah took a sip of her drink. "You aren't going to be taking care of Danny, are you?" The disapproval in her voice was strong.

"That's not what I was hired for," Brittany said angrily. "I'm a nurse and Nate is my patient. You and Ethan will have to decide who takes care of the baby.''

Just then they heard Ethan, Nate and Danny coming back

to the family room. Ethan carried the crying child. "Now what's wrong with him," Hannah asked sulkily. "He's been fussing all day."

"Well, for one thing his diaper's wet," Ethan told her. "Also, he's probably tired and hungry."

"Well that's not my fault," Hannah whined. "I can't do everything at once. The only reason he was happy when I first brought him over here is because you and Nate spoil him to death."

Ethan gently patted the child's back. "Where's what's-her-name? The latest nanny."

"Hayley," Hannah said, supplying the name. "Ungrateful little snip. She packed up and left as soon as I told her I was moving to Chicago. I thought you might want to hire her to take care of Danny over here, but she said something about going to stay with a friend in Los Angeles and took off. She'd planned to give me her notice tomorrow."

Even though she hadn't had much experience with small children, Brittany had always been drawn to them and she could understand why Danny was so upset. The atmosphere in the room was volatile, and even though he wouldn't understand what was being said, the voices raised in anger were chilling.

Her heart went out to the poor little guy, who was sobbing noisily on his daddy's shoulder, and she looked at Ethan.

"If you'll give me a diaper I can change him," she offered.

"Would you?" Ethan asked.

"Sure," she said.

"I'll get them." He left the room to return a few minutes later with a package of disposable diapers and baby wipes.

He walked over to where Brittany was standing and put the box on an end table, then peeled Danny's arms from around his neck and handed him to Brittany.

Danny would have none of that and screamed, "No, Da-da, Da-da" as he held his arms out for Ethan to take him again.

Danny was solid and his kicking and squirming made it hard for Brittany to hold on to him, but she backed away when Ethan tried to take him again.

"No, let me keep him," she said. "If I can wrestle two-hundred-pound men in and out of hospital beds I can surely tame a twenty-five-pound baby."

She picked up the packages and carried them and the child to the other couch. "There now, little guy," she crooned. "Don't be afraid. I just want to put dry pants on you."

She sat down and held Danny over her shoulder the way Ethan had, then lightly massaged his back and talked quietly to him in a reassuring tone. He still sobbed but he was no longer so frantic.

Finally, when Brittany was fairly sure he would submit to her ministrations, she laid him on the couch on his back and unsnapped the inside seam of his blue denim overalls.

She continued to talk to him all the time she worked. There was no conversation in the room. Everyone watched in silence, undoubtedly afraid he'd tune up again if it was broken.

When she finished, she picked him up and sat him on her lap. He waved his arms and grinned. She had the distinct impression that everyone was fighting the urge to break out in applause.

What a ridiculous idea! She'd managed to quiet Danny, but after all she was a nurse and, besides, she had a natural affinity for children.

She looked up at Ethan. "If you want me to I can give him his supper. Nate's overdue for something to eat, too. I'm willing to feed them both while you and Ms. Thorpe put all these baby things away—"

"Sorry, guys, but you're on your own," Hannah said as she stood up. "I have all I can handle getting my own stuff packed and ready to leave."

She turned to face Ethan. "Contact our lawyer and have the necessary papers drawn up transferring custody of Danny from joint to you. I'll sign them. All I ask is reasonable visitation rights.''

She dug her car keys out of her purse. ''My flight leaves at three-thirty tomorrow afternoon. I'll come by on my way to the airport and say goodbye to Danny. Make sure he's available.''

She turned and walked up the hall and out the door.

Brittany sat on the couch with the contented baby on her lap, and Ethan and Nate stood, all three staring after the retreating figure in utter amazement.

''Well I'll be damned,'' Nate gasped. ''Don't that beat all! I never did like that woman, son, but I figured that since she was the one you chose to marry it wasn't up to me to criticize, but now...''

He let the sentence trail off and grabbed the back of the couch Brittany was sitting on with both hands. Brittany caught the movement out of the corner of her eye and instinctively called out ''Catch him'' as Nate wavered back and forth.

The sharpness of her tone set little Danny off again, but Ethan understood the warning and wrapped his arms around his dad's shoulders.

''It's okay, Dad,'' he said soothingly as he steadied Nate and walked him around to the front of the couch.

Brittany stood up with the crying baby in her arms, and Ethan stretched his father out in a reclining position on the sofa. ''You all right now, Dad?'' he asked anxiously.

''I'll get his candy,'' Brittany said, and hurried to the kitchen, still carrying the squalling child, to get a roll of fruit-flavored Life Savers. It was a quick way to bring her patient's blood-sugar level back up to normal and avoid diabetic shock.

When she got back to the family room Ethan stood up and took Danny from her while she sat on the edge of the couch and handed Nate the proper number of candies. While he chewed she kept her hand on the pulse in his wrist and her eyes on the slightly uneven rise and fall of his chest.

"Is he going to be okay?" Ethan asked above the clamor of Danny's sobs.

"Oh, yeah," she assured him. "His blood sugar apparently took a dramatic fall due to the stress of all the upsetting things going on around here, plus he missed his afternoon snack. I was fixing him something to eat when your wife arrived and got everything in an uproar."

"*Ex*-wife," Ethan corrected her.

Brittany got a perverse pleasure out of Ethan's hurry to deny any close relationship with Hannah. How could that woman just abandon their baby like this? It's true her company hadn't given her much time to make a choice between her career and her child, but she could have at least shown a little remorse. Instead she didn't seem to be able to get away fast enough.

"Yes, well whatever," she said, "Nate needs to eat. I noticed you have an assortment of TV dinners in the freezer. Is it okay if I heat some of those in the microwave?"

"I'd appreciate it very much," Ethan answered. "I like roast beef. What will you have, Nate?"

"Fried chicken," Nate said, but before Brittany could protest that deep-fried chicken was filled with fat, Nate continued. "It's a brand especially made for people with dietary restrictions. My doctor has approved it."

She was happy to hear that. "Okay, then, and what does Danny eat?"

"I'll feed him," Ethan said, "while you fix dinner and take care of Dad. There's plenty in the freezer. Take whatever you want for yourself."

"Fine," she said, and looked at Nate. "You stay right there and don't try to get up. It won't take but a few minutes to microwave your frozen chicken. Do you still have black spots in front of your eyes?

He shook his head. "No, that candy did the trick. My hands aren't shaking, either."

* * *

For the next few hours Ethan and Brittany worked unceasingly. Ethan fed Danny, then put away the baby furnishings he needed and carried all the things he had duplicates of, such as high chairs and cribs, down to the basement. Brittany fixed the TV dinners for the three adults and kept an eye on both Nate and his little grandson.

At seven-thirty she caught up with Danny and gave him a bath. He splashed happily in the tub, getting her almost as wet as he was. She rummaged through the chest of drawers in the nursery upstairs and found a pair of pajamas with cartoon characters printed on them. She put them on him and sat down with him in the handmade chair that Ethan told her had rocked several generations of Thorpe babies to sleep.

For a few moments Danny tried to get away from her and play on the floor, but she held on to him firmly and started to sing lullabies as she rocked. In no time he relaxed, put his thumb in his mouth and nestled against her.

Brittany hadn't had much experience with infants and toddlers. She'd done a fair amount of baby-sitting in high school, but her charges had been mostly older children. This little one was pure joy. His skin was so soft, his hair still tousled, and he smelled of soap and baby powder.

She was still humming when she heard a soft sound somewhere between a gasp and a sigh and looked up. There, leaning against the doorjamb, stood Ethan. There were lines of fatigue at the corners of his eyes and mouth and he looked exhausted.

Their gazes locked and clung and wouldn't be torn apart, but it wasn't the magnetism that held her entranced. It was the raw hunger that seemed to look out of his very soul as he watched her cuddle his child.

Chapter Three

Ethan had been in the basement stashing away Danny's surplus things when it occurred to him that he hadn't seen or heard the boy for an uncomfortably long length of time. He'd assumed that Brittany and Nate were taking care of him, but what if they'd thought the same thing about him? They'd all drifted off to various duties without any of them taking specific responsibility for the little guy.

A stab of fear sent Ethan hurrying up to the first floor. There didn't seem to be anybody there, although the television in the family room was going full blast. He turned it off and called Brittany and Nate but there was no answer.

Ordinarily that wouldn't be too alarming since the house was big and tightly built. Also, all the floors except the tiled one in the foyer were heavily carpeted, which pretty much soundproofed the structure. But this was no ordinary situation! He was answerable for his little son now, and he should have been watching him more closely.

Quickly he bounded up the stairs to the second story and took a left turn to check the master bedroom-and-bath suite.

It was empty, but as he neared the nursery next door he heard the soft strains of a lullaby being sung.

He stopped and listened. The melody wasn't familiar, but he knew it wasn't Nate who was singing. This was a woman's voice, sweet and clear.

Ethan crept slowly to the door and looked in. Brittany was sitting in Nate's antique rocking chair cradling Danny in the crook of her arm, his little head pillowed against the curvaceous rise of her breast.

His knees turned rubbery and he leaned against the doorjamb to steady himself. She was the perfect model for a modern-day Madonna, dressed casually in blue jeans and a T-shirt after a long day of work, her lovely young face devoid of makeup and her dark hair falling across her creamy, unblemished cheeks as she bowed her head and lovingly stroked Ethan's sleeping son.

Ethan couldn't help it. He'd fought so valiantly against his desire for her every time he'd seen her these past two weeks, and now she was holding his little boy the way he longed for her to hold him. A moan escaped from deep in his throat and Brittany raised her head.

The singing stopped abruptly, and for a moment she looked startled. Then their gazes locked and hers softened. Ethan knew he should break that hold. He didn't want her to see the depth of emotion she stirred in him, but he couldn't look away. Those big, deep-set green eyes of hers wouldn't let him.

Slowly he started walking across the room, never breaking eye contact, until he stood in front of the chair. She watched him, and when he hunkered down in front of her and murmured, "Let me take him,' she put Danny in his outstretched arms.

As he stood he didn't know where this interlude was going, but he was sure of one thing. She'd have to help get them back on a business-only basis. He couldn't do it alone.

Ethan laid the sleeping youngster in the crib and covered

him with a light blanket, then leaned over and kissed him on the cheek. "Sleep peacefully, son," he whispered.

Ethan straightened and pulled up the side of the crib, then once again turned around to face Brittany. She was still sitting in the chair. He crossed to her and put out his hands. She took them and he pulled her up and into his aching arms.

He breathed a sigh of relief. The pain of wanting her and the strain of denying it had been torture. She was warm and soft and fit against him in all the right places. His self-control shattered and he kissed her, gently at first because of her youth and inexperience. Dear God, she was only twenty-one. He had no business toying with her this way. He was supposed to be the strong one, the adult.

He was trying to gather the strength to remember he was her employer, not her lover, when she opened her mouth and shyly welcomed him. All thoughts of breaking it off disappeared as his tongue caressed hers and he wrapped her in his embrace.

"Oh, Brittany," he groaned. "I'm sorry. This is wrong."

He felt her stiffen, but neither of them made a move to pull apart.

"Why is it wrong?" she asked against his cheek.

He nuzzled her neck. "You know why. I want you so much that I can't keep my hands off you. I've always known you were off limits and even so I'm breaking all the rules."

She tipped her head back and looked at him. "What rules?" She seemed genuinely puzzled. "You said you and Hannah were divorced."

He blinked. "We are. This has nothing to do with Hannah. I'm talking about you. Your age, for one thing. You're so very young."

Her eyes widened. "You don't like young women?"

"I *teach* young women, I don't make love to them."

They'd come to a good lead-in and he might as well bring the question he needed to ask out in the open now and get it over with. "*Are* you experienced, Brittany? Have you ever been with a man?"

For a moment she just looked at him, then she buried her face in his shoulder. "No." It was little more than a whisper. "But I've never before met one I wanted to be...um...*with* in that way."

Pride and regret warred within him. He was proud of her for waiting to have that momentous experience until she met the man she considered the right one, and he deeply regretted that he wasn't and could never be that person.

He brushed her hair away from her cheek. "I'm flattered that you think I might be that man," he murmured into her ear. "I wish I were, but I'm afraid I'm not. Shall we go downstairs to the family room and talk about it?"

She nodded but made no move to pull away from him, and the very thought of letting her go was intolerable. What harm could it do if he held her for just a little while longer? Now that he knew she was attracted to him, too, they could bring their mutual enticement out into the open and deal with it.

With his left arm he turned her so she could walk along beside him while he hugged her close to his side. As they made their way down the stairs, across the foyer and along the hall to the family room, Ethan belatedly remembered his father.

"Where's Nate?" he asked Brittany. "I haven't seen him—"

"He went to bed early," she said. "He was pretty well worn out after all the upheaval this afternoon and evening."

Ethan seated her on the sofa and dimmed the lights.

"Would you like something to drink?" he asked.

She nodded. "I'd like a cola if you have one."

He smiled. "Coming right up." He headed for the kitchen.

A few minutes later he returned with two glasses and handed one to her. He set the other one on the coffee table and lowered himself down beside her so close that their hips and thighs touched. That was a mistake he hadn't intended to make, but he had and he wasn't going to rectify it now. Her soft flesh against his was too alluring for him to deprive himself of the pleasure unless she objected.

She didn't, and he leaned forward and picked up his glass of vodka and water. He needed something to fortify his fractured nervous system if he ever hoped to keep his wits about him and behave like a gentleman instead of a lusting adolescent.

Brittany locked her fingers around the glass of soda to steady her hands and keep from spilling the contents. She was totally overcome by Ethan's kiss. Although she'd often dreamed of it happening, she'd thought her feelings had all been one-sided. Until tonight he'd never shown any sign of even liking her let alone being attracted to her. Although they'd only known each other for two weeks, she'd been drawn to him from the minute they'd met.

He put his arm around her shoulders and snuggled her against him. She relaxed and laid her head on his chest. "You were saying," she murmured.

"I don't remember," he admitted as he rained tiny kisses on the top of her head. "All I can think of is the taste of your lips, the scent of baby powder on your hands, and the way our bodies fit together as if they were made for each other."

She liked the sound of that. "Maybe they were." Her voice was little more than a whisper. Should she come right out and say what she was thinking? All her girlfriends let the guys know when they were willing to sleep with them. The women claimed the fellows liked having them take the initiative. It made men feel macho, pumped up their ego and started the testosterone flowing.

Her more-experienced women friends teased her about her reluctance to have sex with a man as opposed to making love with one. To make love you had to be in love, and Ethan was the only one she'd ever felt that strongly about.

Well, nothing ventured nothing gained, as her grandpa always used to say. She cleared her throat. "I…I guess we could always find out. That is…"

She felt him tense and knew she'd made a mistake. She was being much too forward. She'd been propositioned many times, but she'd never come on to a man before.

Ethan didn't seem pleased, even though it was all too evident that he wanted her.

She stirred and raised her head to look at him. His face was expressionless and the hot swell of humiliation surged through her. "I…I'm sorry," she said, and tried to stand up, but he grabbed her by the wrist and pulled her back down. "You must think I'm a real…a real…"

"That's enough," he said angrily as he refused to let her loose. Don't you ever let me hear you call yourself disrespectful names."

"I only wanted to let you know…" Her voice broke and she couldn't go on.

"I know what you wanted to let me know, honey," he told her softly, "and I didn't answer you right away because I was fighting off an overpowering urge to sweep you into my arms and carry you upstairs to bed."

He hugged her close. "On the other hand, I've got to warn you, don't ever come on to a man unless you're prepared to carry through."

She sighed and relaxed again in his arms. "I was prepared to carry through, but telling you was a mistake I've never made before and will never make again. You didn't like it, I could tell."

"I loved it," he told her, "but I don't think you realized how difficult it is for me not to take you up on your offer. A lot of men would simply have taken advantage of your innocence and then blamed you for 'leading them on' when the experience was unsatisfactory for you.''

He tipped her face up and rubbed her nose with his own. "Some day you'll thank me for not taking your virginity. Save that precious first time for the man you truly love."

She pressed her cheek against his. His five-o'clock beard was bristly but endearing. "Why are you so sure you're not that man?"

He paused as if gathering his thoughts, then answered. "Because I'm all wrong for you. You've only recently lost your parents and you're alone and vulnerable. You're looking for a father figure, and who better than me? Although, I'm a little young for that role."

She drew in a breath to protest but he hurried on. "Factor in Nate as a perfect grandfather model and Danny, whom you could grow to love like a son, and you've got a family again. What you feel for me is security, possible infatuation, but you need a young man you can grow up with, not a middle-aged one who comes from a different generation."

Brittany turned and put her palm flat on his shoulder, then pushed herself away from him. "That is the most ridiculous thing I ever heard," she said angrily. "I suggest you're the one who needs to grow up. I think you're afraid of me."

"Damn right I am!" he admitted even as he gathered her back in his arms. "I'd be a fool not to be. Try to understand, honey. I'm a college professor and you've been a student at the university where I teach. You'll probably return there to finish your education sometime soon, which would make a romantic relationship between us pretty dicey. But that's not the biggest problem. I'll be thirty-six years old in a few months, I was married for eight years and have an eighteen-month-old child who needs constant supervision. I also have a dependent father. Don't you see? You don't want my problems. You need a new, young family of your own."

She sighed and snuggled deeper into his embrace. This was

getting them nowhere. "I don't want to argue anymore, let's change the subject. What are you going to do about Danny tomorrow?"

Ah, yes, Danny, Ethan thought. He'd been so busy trying to explain to Brittany why he didn't want her, when they both knew he did, that he hadn't had time to make any plans for coping with the upheaval having his baby son full-time would cause in his life.

"I don't know," he admitted. "I'll need to take the day off and try to find either a baby-sitter or a child-care center that has room for him. There's one at the university but I understand it's always filled to capacity. I'll have to have someone by Monday because that's when we start preparing for finals at school and I have to be there."

A solution occurred to Brittany. "Why don't you let me take care of him tomorrow? I'll be here anyway, and that will free you up to spend your time looking for a permanent situation for Danny."

"But you've got a full-time job taking care of Nate," Ethan reminded her.

She raised her head and looked at him. "Nate's no bother. Mainly all I have to do is make sure he gets his meds on time and eats regularly. That will leave me plenty of time to look after Danny. As long as they don't get out of the house or the fenced-in backyard it should be a breeze."

Ethan smiled sadly. Ah, the innocence of the young! "Obviously you've never been around children much. Especially ones Danny's age. They can be adorable little brats and usually are. You got a taste of it this afternoon, but you'd have a whole day of chasing after him all by yourself tomorrow.

Brittany was getting tired of being treated as if she were dim-witted. She moved out of his embrace and sat up. "Look, if you don't trust me with your child just say so. I'm willing to help you out if you need it, but I'm not going to beg."

She stood and went to the closet where she kept her purse.

"I'm going home and do some laundry before I go to bed. You make up your mind what you want to do and let me know in the morning."

She picked up her purse and was almost to the door when she heard Ethan call her name. It would have given her a great deal of satisfaction to stomp out and slam the door behind her, but that would only prove she was as immature as he thought she was.

Instead she stopped but didn't turn to look at him.

"I would be very grateful if you would take care of Danny as well as Nate tomorrow." His voice was husky. "Thank you for offering. It will be an immense help."

Although she had her back to him, she could hear his footsteps on the tile floor as he approached her. He stopped right behind her, took her shoulders in his hands and turned her to face him.

"Now, do I get a good-night kiss?" he asked hopefully.

Without a word she put her arms around his neck and their lips melded.

During the long weekend Ethan learned, much to his distress, that finding child care in Lexington, Kentucky, was impossible. The care centers, both public and private, were filled and had long waiting lists. Mothers who stayed at home and took care of their own children weren't interested in taking in the kids of strangers, too. Students with summer holidays coming up were, in his judgment, either too immature to be trusted with such a young child or preferred to play around for the next three months before going off to college in the fall.

Surely somewhere in this city of more than 200,000 people there was one who fit his admittedly high standards as a nanny.

That thought sounded dumb even to him. Of course there was such a person and he'd known who it was since before he'd started this search. Brittany could satisfy all his needs.

The perfect nanny for Danny, nurse for Nate, and lover for him.

A shiver ran down his spine. What more could he want? He was almost certain she'd agree to be nanny and nurse. Being his lover might take a little persuasion, but she'd already told him she'd like to make love with him, so why did he hesitate?

Because he wasn't that kind of man, dammit! He couldn't take advantage of a young girl's naiveté, and she was a girl no matter how much she protested that she was all grown-up. He might burn for her but that was his problem. It was up to him to protect her, even from himself if necessary, and he couldn't do that if she was living right here in the same house with him.

My God, he wasn't a saint!

Brittany's phone rang late on Sunday evening. It was Ethan. She hadn't heard from him since she left his house to come home Friday night, but she'd been thinking of him all weekend.

He sounded tired and discouraged. "Brittany, I have a big favor to ask of you. Is your offer to take care of Danny on a temporary basis still open?"

So he hadn't had any luck finding child care yet. "Of course it is, Ethan," she hurriedly assured him. "Nate and I are going to take a picnic lunch and go to the park tomorrow. We'll find one that has a children's playground. Danny will love that."

"I'm sure he will, but can you keep track of them both at the same time?" She could hear the anxiety in his tone.

"Oh, sure," she said. "Nate always stays close by me when we go out together, and Danny still needs hands-on help to play on the playground equipment. He and his grandpa will get along great together, and I'll be right there every minute."

"Well, if you're certain…" Ethan said, but Brittany could hear the doubt in his tone. It was going to take a while for him to feel comfortable about the responsibility of having full-time care of his toddler.

"Ethan, if you're uneasy about this picnic I'll cancel it," she offered. "I don't want you to worry all day about your family when you're in the middle of giving tests—"

"No. No, that's all right," he insisted. "Don't change your plans. Nate loves to get out on days when the weather is as beautiful as it's been lately, and Danny screams with delight when he flies down the slide or goes around on the small carousel. I'm just and old worrywart—"

"You're a caring father," she said softly, "and I wouldn't have you any other way. Why don't you come and have lunch with us? I can bring extra food—"

"I wish I could," he said regretfully, "but I'm scheduled right through the lunch period. School will be out soon, though, and then I'll have a break before the summer classes start."

Brittany was surprised. "Do you teach in the summer, too? Don't you ever take a vacation?"

He laughed. "Now and then I grab a couple of days," he joked, but then his tone turned serious. "It probably won't pay for me to work during the summer after this year now that I have to hire caregivers for both Nate and Danny. Besides, I don't want my son raised by strangers no matter how efficient they might be. I want to spend as much time with him as I possibly can."

Brittany flinched. So that's why he wouldn't let her care for Danny. Not because he thought it was too much work for her, but because he still considered her a stranger and therefore not good enough to take charge of his child.

"I see," she said, and there was a distinct chill in her tone. "Then I'll see you in the morning."

She put the phone in the cradle and broke the connection before he could say more.

* * *

The search for child care stretched out past the next day to the full week and culminated in Ethan agreeing to hire Brittany on a temporary full-time basis until he could find someone else to take over the position. She was given a substantial raise in pay, but Ethan kept their relationship on a strictly employer-employee bases.

There was no more touching, or hugging, or kissing, and he politely discouraged her from staying around when he got home in the afternoon.

She wished he'd just ask her to stay for dinner some evening or go to a movie with him, but he never indicated in any way that he wanted to date her. Brittany hated it, but knew it was the only possible way they could work together without compromising their moral values. She'd never be any man's mistress, not even Ethan's, and it wasn't hard to stay true to that resolution since he had never asked her to be.

Also, she was well aware of the fact that he'd never brought the word *marriage* into the conversation.

She'd sure lost no time breaking one of the most fundamental rules of nursing. *Don't get personally involved with your patient!* Yeah. Sure. She adored Nate and it hadn't taken long to figure out that she was also passionately in love with his son.

Some nurse she turned out to be!

The school year was winding down, and reluctantly Ethan asked Brittany if it would be possible for her to baby-sit Danny and Nate on the nights when he, as a member of the faculty, was expected to attend various functions at the university.

"I wouldn't ask you if I could find anyone else to do it," he apologized, "but they've called a special faculty meeting at school tonight and I really have to be there. Unfortunately, the elderly woman who usually comes over to play cards with Nate when I have to got out after dinner has recently moved to Frankfort to live with her daughter. Besides, she'd never be able to handle Danny. I will, of course, pay you overtime.''

"I'd be happy to stay with them," Brittany told him. "What time do you want me to come back?''

It was on the tip of her tongue to tell him he didn't need to pay her at all, much less overtime, but she resisted. He'd made it plain in the weeks she'd been here that their relationship was to be strictly professional. She wasn't going to make the mistake again of baring her true feelings for him.

He looked at his watch. "It's five-thirty now and the meeting starts at seven-thirty. That hardly leaves you time to go home and come back again.''

He hesitated. "Why don't you stay here and have dinner with us? We'll make it a family affair. I fixed spaghetti sauce last night so I'll cook the pasta, you can toss a salad and Nate can warm up the French bread.''

Brittany's heart was pounding with excitement. *We'll make it a family affair.* She wondered if he understood what he'd said and how deeply it had affected her.

At last he was making friendly gestures toward her. He'd not only invited her to dinner, but he was even going to let her take part in preparing the meal instead of treating her like a guest.

"I'd love to," she told him, trying to control her elation. "I make a mean salad.''

Brittany watched unobtrusively as Nate wrapped the French bread in aluminum foil and stuck it in the oven, then put Danny in his high chair and spooned baby food into his eager little mouth. The child pounded on the tray with his hands and squealed with delight while Nate teased him by offering then withdrawing the small spoon.

Ever since she'd been taking care of Danny, Brittany had been amazed at the dexterity with which Nate handled the little one. He seemed to know exactly how to cater to Danny without spoiling him, and play with him without losing his own bearings.

Nate must have been a wonderful father to Ethan and Peter. Brittany envied the twins. Ethan seemed so sure that she was confusing her feelings for him with those of a girl looking for a father, but she knew without doubt that was not true. She loved Ethan like a woman loves a lover. A husband.

But he'd gotten one thing right. She loved Nate as deeply as she'd loved her grandfather, who died when she was ten years old. She'd give anything if Nate could be her grandpa.

They'd eaten in the formal dining room at the front of the house, and Brittany leaned back in her chair and sighed. "That was a delicious meal. You guys are really good cooks."

"We didn't have much choice," Nate said sadly. "After my wife died it was either cook or starve. I bought a cookbook and learned first then taught the boys. Ethan and I are fairly proficient as long as we keep to simple, old-fashioned recipes, but once Pete moved to New Orleans and got a taste of that Cajun style, he branched out and now could hold his own as a chef."

Brittany was still surprised that Nate's long-term memory was so good. It was the short-term one that gave him trouble.

"Any chance I could get you to teach me?" she asked to fill up the silence that seemed to be stretching out too long. "My parents were high powered professionals and we ate out a lot. Even when she did cook, mom wouldn't let me in the kitchen. She said I was clumsy and got in her way...."

This conversation was getting maudlin and she certainly didn't want that. Before she could change the subject, Ethan looked at his watch and pushed back his chair. "Sorry, I hate to break up the party, but it's getting late and I'm going to have to leave."

He started stacking the dirty dishes as she jumped up to help. "You go ahead and get ready, Ethan. Nate and I will do the dishes. After all, you cooked, it's only fair that we clean up.''

"You cooked, too," he reminded her. "Nate can load the dishwater, can't you Dad." It was a statement, not a question.

"Sure," Nate said with a grin. "I'll do that while Brittany chases Danny down and gives him his bath. Her pretty legs are a lot more limber than mine."

Ethan smiled but Brittany thought she saw a touch of envy in his eyes. "Okay, have fun, you two," he said as he walked toward the door.

The following day when Ethan got back to his classroom after lunch he found a memorandum on his desk advising him that a meeting had been called of the instructors in his department for seven-thirty.

He stared at it in disbelief. What in hell was going on! He thought they'd gotten all business regarding graduation taken care of at the meeting the night before. Now they were calling all those in the English department back again.

He balled the note and threw it in the wastebasket. Well, tough luck! They'd have to meet without him. No way was he going to ask Brittany to baby-sit after her regular hours again! Besides, he couldn't afford it. Paying her to take care of both Nate and Danny was rapidly draining his resources.

He sat down in his chair behind the desk and rubbed his hands over his face. Not that she'd asked for the amount he was giving her. In fact, she'd insisted it was too much, but after the research he'd done while trying to find a permanent caregiver he knew that, on the contrary, she was being underpaid.

Reaching for the phone, he punched the number he wanted, but the conversation was short and sweet. He initiated it by telling Grady Ellison, head of the English department, that he couldn't possibly come to the meeting that evening.

"Did someone in the family die?" Grady asked crisply.

"No," Ethan said, "but I—"

"Is your little boy in pediatric ICU at the hospital?" Grady asked again.

"No, dammit, Grady—"

"Has you house burned down since I saw you last night?" The other man's tone was sharp and caustic.

"For God's sake, Grady—" Ethan had had about enough of this. "If you'll just shut up and let me tell you—"

"No, *you* shut up and let me tell you," Grady snarled. "Those are the only excuses I'll accept for not attending. Since none of them has happened to you I don't want to hear any more about it. This is a situation that has come up since last night, and I need every one of you there."

Grady's phone slammed down in Ethan's ear. The conversation was obviously over!

Chapter Four

Ethan cursed under his breath as he slung books and papers around on his usually neat desk, hunting for the small phone number book he carried with him.

Where was the damn thing now when he needed it? And how was he going to scare up a baby-sitter who was agreeable to taking care of a baby and a sick old man on six hours' notice?

No, wait, that wasn't fair. Danny wasn't exactly a baby. More of a toddler. And Nate was certainly not sick and old. He was an elderly gentleman who had a few health problems, but even so Ethan had been through all the names in his book in his search for permanent help, some several times, and none of them were either able or willing to take on that responsibility.

Then he remembered. A couple of weeks ago he'd bought a box of cookies from a student in his American Lit class. Her name was Anna something and she was selling them for her little sister who was a Girl Scout. She'd seemed like a really nice, intelligent young woman, and he remembered asking her at the time if she'd be interested in applying for the job of baby-sitting his son during the summer session, but she said she was leaving as soon as school was out to spend the summer with her grandparents in Wisconsin.

Maybe she'd be free tonight!

Ordinarily he'd never approach a female student on campus to ask for a favor or offer employment. He had run a Help Wanted ad in the school paper but hadn't had any responses.

This time, though, he was desperate. He had a good reputation as an instructor and never dated or got personal with any of the students, not even the older ones who were returning to get their degrees after dropping out of school for one reason or another. Surely no one would misconstrue a simple cry for help by baby-sitting his little son for a couple of hours.

It took a while but Ethan finally located Anna Whiteside in one of the math classes and explained his problem to her. "I know this is putting you on the spot," he concluded, "and believe me I'd never do it if the situation weren't crucial."

"Gee, Mr. Thorpe. I'd like to help you out, I really would," she said, and sounded sincere, "but I've already promised Mom and Dad I'd baby-sit my little brother and sister tonight so they can go to the Stones concert."

Ethan wrinkled his brow. "The what?"

Anna laughed. "The Rolling Stones. I guess you weren't part of the subculture of the late sixties and early seventies. Neither was I, obviously, since I wasn't born until 1980, but Mom and Dad really flipped when they found out the Rolling Stones were coming back."

Ethan cleared his throat. "Oh, yes, I remember reading something about that. I was never into rock and roll."

Ethan felt like a fool. Apparently, he was even further behind the times than he'd thought. He remembered his middle and high school years and the racket Peter and his friends had called music, but Ethan had preferred classical and jazz when he bothered to listen at all. He'd always been an avid reader and spent most of his leisure time with his nose in a book.

All that reading had paid off in their college years. He'd sailed through his classes and also spent a lot of time tutoring Pete in the subjects in which he'd fallen behind. Fortunately his twin brother was a quick study and made excellent grades all through law school.

"I'm afraid I have to plead guilty to being unfamiliar with rock and roll bands," Ethan admitted, "but I'm sure your parents have excellent taste and will enjoy the concert. Thanks, anyway."

He turned and started to leave but she called to him. "Professor Thorpe, if you'd like to bring your little boy over to my house I can watch him there. My brother and sister are eight and ten, old enough to help entertain him."

Ethan was elated. By a happy coincidence her family lived in the same general area of town as he did, and he'd already decided to take Nate to the meeting with him so he hadn't even mentioned his dad to the girl. This would work out just great and he wouldn't have to bother Brittany again!

Several hours later, at seven-fifteen, Ethan parked his car in his space in the parking lot, then assisted his dad into the building and the room where the meeting was taking place. It was a faculty lounge-conference room with a large rectangular table and numerous fold-up chairs in the center and two comfortable chairs with reading lamps in the corners at the back.

Ethan introduced his father to those in the assembled group who hadn't already met him, then seated him in one of the chairs at the back.

"Are you comfortable now, Dad?" he asked as he handed Nate the book he'd brought along, then turned on the lamp. "Is there anything else you'd like?"

"I'm fine, son," Nate assured him. "Now, don't you worry about me. I'll just sit here and read."

"Okay. If you need anything just come and get me. I'll be sitting right there at the table." Ethan had no qualms about his father's welfare, and he took his place at the table just as Grady Ellison banged his gavel.

The discussion concerned a number of last-minute changes in the summer curriculum. From time to time Ethan remembered Nate and glanced over to make sure he was all right. He was always reading and looked perfectly content.

As the discussion became more heated, the professors demanded that more attention be given to their diverse points of view, until one of them announced that it was almost eleven o'clock and she'd promised to get her baby-sitter home by now.

Everyone was dismayed to hear it was so late and started stuffing papers and pamphlets into their briefcases and rushing for the exit. It was almost an hour later than Ethan had estimated he'd be picking up Danny. He hoped Anna, and her parents if they were home yet, wouldn't be concerned.

Ethan was one of the few left when he finished getting his things together and looked across the room at Nate.

Only he didn't see his dad. All he saw was an empty chair bathed in the light from the lamp!

For a moment Ethan was too startled to react. *Hold on there,* he told himself, *don't panic. He can't be too far away.*

A cold shiver ran down his spine and he called out. "Dad. Dad, where are you? We're going home now."

There was no response, but the sound of his own voice in the empty room galvanized his legs into action and he ran. Fortunately he was familiar with the layout of the building and knew exactly where he was going as he raced up and down the twisted hallways opening doors and calling Nate's name.

By this time everyone was gone except Quinn, the night janitor, who caught up with Ethan and offered his help as soon as he realized something was wrong. Quickly Ethan explained the situation and they each went in different directions shout-

ing and turning lights on in hopes that Nate would find his
way to them even if he was having a panic attack and didn't
know who or where he was.

All the time Ethan searched, he berated himself for not paying closer attention to his father. He'd been so secure in the
knowledge that Nate was right there in the room with him,
would even have to pass beside the table where Ethan was
seated in order to get to the door if he wanted to leave, that
he'd let his guard down.

How could he have let Grady Ellison badger him into attending this meeting when he had family emergencies at
home? They couldn't fire Ethan, he had tenure, and they
couldn't force him to work more than a certain number of
hours overtime. He'd put those in months ago and had hours
to spare.

If anything happened to Nate…

Ethan couldn't bear to think about that now.

When Quinn and Ethan caught up with each other again
they agreed that Nate had possibly left the building and was
wandering around outside somewhere. The idea was terrifying,
but they couldn't waste any time. Nate lost all sense of direction when he got confused.

Ethan put in a quick call to Anna to brief her on the situation and ask her to keep Danny overnight at her house if
necessary. She agreed, and with that worry off his mind he
suggested to Quinn that he stay in the building and continue
to search there while he, Ethan, would walk around outside
and, if necessary, take his car to explore a wider range. If only
he knew how long his dad had been gone before Ethan missed
him!

The police department didn't consider a person officially
missing until he or she had been gone for forty-eight hours,
but they might make an exception in Nate's case since he had
a medical problem. As a last resort he'd call 911.

Quinn turned on the outside lights on the school building

and found a large flashlight for Ethan, but even so it was difficult to see in the dark shadows and nooks and crannies where the light didn't reach. The first place he looked was his car, but no luck. He continued to call out Nate's name and stood under streetlights as much as possible so his dad could see him, but the silence between his calls was deafening.

Finally, Ethan took his car and started driving around the campus, but there was no one on the streets, either walking or driving.

Suddenly a thought occurred to him. Brittany's apartment was only two or three blocks from the campus. Ethan had never been there, but she'd told him about it. It was in a large old house and most of the tenants were students.

Could she have taken Nate there at some time, maybe to pick up something she needed, and he remembered? Was it possible he was trying to find her?

Immediately Ethan pulled over to the curb and reached for his cell phone.

Brittany was having trouble sleeping. She'd been tired when she went to bed, but since then she'd tossed and turned and couldn't seem to rest. Something was bothering her but she didn't know what it was. If she were prone to premonition she'd think that was it, but no one was more earthbound than she. She needed good solid proof before she believed anything she couldn't see.

She pulled the sheet over her shoulders and had just started to relax when the shrill ring of the telephone cut through the silence of the room. Oh, for heaven's sake, who would be calling her at this time of night? It had to be close to midnight.

She reached for the phone on the bedside table, but then realized it was her cell phone. Darn! If she got out of bed and headed across the room to get it out of her purse, then talked to the caller, even if it was just a wrong number, which she was sure it was, she'd be hours getting to sleep.

Maybe she'd just let it ring. Why not? There was no law saying you had to answer your telephone.

It rang again, and again, and again, each time escalating her curiosity and her guilt. Finally she could stand it no longer and got out of bed, only to have the ringing stop while she was searching for her purse.

"Damn!" she muttered as she finally spied it on the floor beside her reclining chair. Now she'd probably spend the rest of the night wondering who it was and what they'd wanted.

She took the cell phone out of her purse and carried it back to bed with her. She would put it on the nightstand so she wouldn't have to get up again if whoever it had been called back.

She'd just climbed into bed when the thing went off in her hand, startling her so that she almost threw it. Quickly she punched it on and spoke petulantly into it. "Look, whoever you are, I'm trying to sleep. Can't this wait till morning?"

"I'm sorry," said a voice that she recognized instantly as Ethan's, "but I need to know if you've seen or heard from Nate?"

"Ethan! What's the matter?" Her heart was racing. "I thought you were a wrong number. What's happened to Nate?"

"I can't find him," Ethan explained, and she could hear the fear in his voice. "I was hoping maybe he'd contacted you. Have you seen or heard from him in the last hour?"

How had Ethan's dad gotten away from him? Especially at this time of night. "No. Why would I? Isn't he home with you?"

"I'm not at home. I'm calling from my car phone at the corner of…" He hesitated, apparently checking the street signs under the light, then gave her the names.

What he was saying didn't make sense. Why was he in that area of town at this time of night? "What are you doing on the campus?"

"I had to come back for another meeting tonight..." he began, and filled her in on all the events that had transpired since he'd been notified of the emergency meeting.

"But why didn't you tell me you had to go out again?" she asked impatiently. "I would have stayed with Nate and Danny."

"I know you would have, honey, but I didn't want to inconvenience you—"

"I don't ever want to hear those words from you again," she scolded, "and I'll have more to say on the subject later, but first we have to find Nate. I'll take my car and scour my neighborhood. I'm familiar with it. You continue to search the campus, and we'll keep in touch with our cell phones."

Brittany broke the connection and, pulling on a pair of jeans and a sweatshirt, rushed outside to her car. She wasn't too concerned yet about Nate's physical condition. She'd seen to it that he had his medication, meals and snacks on time all day, and he carried his candy on him everywhere he went, so what really bothered her was the possibility that if he was disoriented and wandering around in the dark alone he might step out in the road and get hit by a car, or be mugged.

She drove slowly and turned her lights on bright as she steered the auto down the middle of the empty street. Every few yards she stopped and called his name out the open window, then waited before starting up again.

It seemed unlikely to her that he'd get this far away from the building where Ethan said the meeting had been held. He'd have to walk almost halfway across the dimly lit campus and then find his way through the thick stand of moss-covered trees that surrounded it. If he managed to do that he'd be even more lost than before because the houses on this side of the university where she lived all looked pretty much alike, big, two story, with numerous steps leading to the front door.

She'd been driving up one street and down another for about ten minutes with no luck when she thought she saw something moving on the right side of the road. She couldn't be sure because it was so dark, but she thought it was a figure weaving back and forth on the sidewalk.

Excitement mounting, she pulled over closer to the curb and shone her headlights in the direction she'd been facing. Sure enough there was the figure of a tall man stumbling ahead of her car! Was it Nate? All she could see was his back, but it must be him. Please, God, let it be him!

She slammed on her brakes and honked her horn. "Nate!" she called out her open window. "Nate, it's Brittany! Wait for me."

He didn't stop but staggered on. Her first inclination was to stop the car and go after him, but she was well aware of how dangerous it was for a woman to accost a strange man on the streets in the middle of the night.

"Sir. Sir, please stop even if your name's not Nate," she called. "I want to talk to you."

All of her doors were locked so she'd be safe enough even if he wasn't Nate, but she needed to know one way or the other. The way he walked scared her. He may just be a drunk looking for another bar, but it could be Nate on the verge of diabetic shock. Diabetics were often mistaken for drunks.

She'd never seen the dress slacks and sport coat this man was wearing, but around the house Nate dressed comfortably in jeans or baggy slacks and pullover knit shirts. That didn't mean he wouldn't dress up when he went out. Especially if he went to a meeting with his son.

He continued to veer down the sidewalk while paying no attention to the car or Brittany's frantic efforts to gain his attention. Finally she could wait no longer. She had to get out of the car and go after him. She was strong and this man was obviously drunk or sick. She was almost sure it was Nate, in which case she'd have nothing to fear, but even if it was a stranger he needed help.

First, though, she'd call for backup. She grabbed her phone

and punched Ethan's number while still letting the car roll along beside the person. It was answered at once by a frantic Ethan.

"I think I've found Nate," she said quickly. "Tell me what he was wearing."

Ethan described his father's clothes and she breathed a sigh of relief. It was Nate, all right. She explained what was happening and told him she was going to confront the man.

"I'm on my way," he assured her. "Be careful, Brittany, you could still be mistaken."

"I know," she said, "but I don't think I am. See you in a few minutes."

She pulled over to the curb, set the brake and jumped out of the car, again calling Nate's name. He kept on walking, but she ran and caught up with him. "Nate, is that you?" she asked as she grabbed his upper arms and turned him so she could see his face.

Relief washed over her as she looked into his familiar features.

"Brittany?" His expression crumbled and he wrapped his arms around her. "Oh, Brittany, I'm lost. I can't find my way."

She could feel his whole body trembling as they held each other, and she knew she had to get him home and medicated as quickly as possible.

"You're not lost any longer," she assured him as she held him close. "I'm here now and Ethan is coming. We're going to take you home. Do you have your candy with you?"

"Yeah, it's in my coat pocket," he said.

She reached into his pocket, brought out a roll of hard candy and gave him the required amount.

"Now, my car is right back there." She pointed to it. "Can you walk that far if I help you?"

"Sh...sure," he said, but she noticed the slurring of the word.

She could walk back and drive the auto to him. It was only about half a block, but she was afraid if she left him standing here with no support he'd collapse.

"Okay, then, just lean on me and we'll be there in no time."

With their arms around each other's waist they started the slow journey. Nate needed a lot of support and he was heavy, but eventually they reached their destination. Brittany more or less dumped him into the front passenger seat, making sure his arm and leg were clear, then buckled him in and closed the door.

By this time Ethan had just pulled up behind her and got out of his car. "Is it Dad?" he asked as he sprinted around to the passenger side and reopened the door.

"Yes," she said. "He's exhausted and upset but—"

"Have you called 911?" Ethan interrupted.

"No, not yet," she told him. "I will if you want me to, but I'm pretty sure I can take care of him. We'll have to get him home quickly, though. I'm afraid a trip to the emergency room would just be more upsetting and cause his blood sugar to go down even further."

"Well, if you're certain..." His voice trailed off.

"No, I'm not certain," she confessed, "but this has already been an extremely stressful experience. I don't want to put him through more if we can help it. If he were my father I'd wait awhile and see how he does. However, this is your decision and I'll go along with whatever you decide."

Ethan paused and Brittany remembered another option she had. "I almost forgot, I can call the twenty-four-hour information hot line my medical service provides. You can trust them. They're doctors and RNs. They'll tell us what to do."

"Brittany, it's not that I don't trust you—"

"I know," she assured him, "but let's do it this way, then we'll both be reassured."

Ethan hunkered down and started talking softly to his father while Brittany put in a call to her hot line. After she'd talked to the RN on duty, explaining the situation and giving them all the vitals she had available, the nurse agreed with Brittany's proposed course of action. Brittany then handed the phone to Ethan so he could speak to the nurse.

"Okay, that's good enough for me," he said, then handed Brittany back the phone. "I'll stop at the Whitesides and pick up Danny then meet you at home." He headed back to his car and she slid under the steering wheel of hers.

When they got home, Danny was asleep so Ethan put the child's pajamas on him and laid him in his crib while Brittany tended to Nate. It was almost an hour later before everything was taken care of and they could ask Nate a few simple questions. He was ready for bed and lying on the couch in the family room where they could watch him for any negative reactions that hadn't shown up yet when Ethan asked, "Dad, why did you leave the meeting? I remember telling you to come and get me if you got tired or..."

"I was just looking for the men's room," Nate said. "It seemed silly for me to bother you and interrupt your meeting when I could just as well find it on my own—"

"But that's the problem," Ethan countered. "You couldn't."

"Oh, I found it okay," Nate insisted, "but when I came out I must have taken a wrong turn because I kept walking and walking but I couldn't find the meeting room. Then I started to panic and I got more and more confused...."

Brittany could see that he was becoming distraught and shook her head lightly at Ethan as she spoke. "It's all right. The way those old buildings are laid out it's a wonder anybody can find the classroom they're looking for. Now, I think it's time for you to go to bed. It's very late, so try to sleep a long time in the morning. Okay?"

Ethan got up and helped his dad to stand. "Take my arm,

Dad," he said, and linked Nate's arm to his own. "I'll tuck you in. You're still a little shaky."

Nate's grin was somewhat tremulous but Brittany saw the familiar mischief in his eyes. "I'd rather she did it." He nodded toward Brittany.

"No way," Ethan said. "Get your own girl, this one's mine."

They all laughed and the two men started up the stairs, but Brittany was too surprised to move. She knew they were just kidding each other, but was it possible there could have been a grain of truth in what Ethan said?

Get your own girl, this one's mine.

She knew Nate was clowning around. They were always giving each other a hard time, and neither of them took it seriously. But Ethan was another matter. He was more serious, more inclined not to talk unless he had something to say.

He'd never teased her the way his father did, and sometimes she got the feeling that he disapproved of their lighthearted banter.

She was jarred out of her musing by Ethan's voice calling to her from the second-floor landing. "Brittany, you don't have to leave yet, do you? Can we talk for a while? If you'd like to fix some hot chocolate I'll only be a few minutes."

"I'd be happy to," she called back eagerly. No way was she going to miss the opportunity to find out what he had in mind.

She was in the kitchen pouring chocolate syrup into mugs of hot milk when he returned. She heard him on the stairs but wasn't prepared for it when he came up behind her and put his arms around her waist. "What would I ever do without you?" he asked huskily as he rubbed his face in her hair.

His touch was just as intoxicating as she'd remembered it to be, and she leaned against him as his arms tightened. "I—I don't know what you mean," she stammered. "I didn't do anything that anyone else wouldn't have done."

"You're always there when I need you." He moved his head to nuzzle the side of her neck, sending chills up and down her spine.

"Mmm, you smell like soap." His tone was little more than a whisper.

She shivered as his mouth continued its foray into the hollow between her neck and shoulder. "I took a shower just before I went to bed." Her voice quivered.

"I wish I'd been there to take it with you," he murmured as he sucked on her earlobe. Waves of heat radiated through her body.

She couldn't hold back. "So do I," she said raggedly, and turned in his arms.

"Oh, Brittany," he groaned, and pushed her groin against his arousal, shooting flames of fire into places she hadn't known had nerves. "You're driving me crazy. Do you know that?"

That did shock her and she shook her head. "No, I didn't. I wasn't even sure you liked me."

The sound he made was a cross between disbelief and a sob. "You little goose, ignoring you was the only way I could keep my sanity. Now that you know how I feel, I don't know how I'm going to resist you."

She pulled back, although still within the circle of his arms, and looked at him. "But I *don't* know how you feel about me," she confessed. "I can't read your mind."

For a moment their gazes locked, but then he put his hand to the back of her head and guided it to his shoulder. "No, I don't suppose you do," he said sadly, "although I find it hard to believe you can be so naive—"

"I'm not naive, Ethan," she said against his chest. "I know how babies are made and I know the difference between love, lust and gratitude. But you keep sending me mixed signals."

"I—I don't know what you mean," he stammered.

"Sure you do," she contradicted him. "Sometimes you

come on to me like you are now, then other times you ignore me. I never know what you want. It's not difficult for any pretty woman to arouse a man sexually. It doesn't even have to be deliberate. It's part of the cycle of life, a way to keep all species re-creating themselves. That's lust.''

"I'll agree with that," he said, "but—"

"And tonight you're grateful to me for helping you find Nate," she continued before he could protest. "You're in a highly emotional state but it's induced by passion, not love. That's gratitude.''

He brushed her hair away from her cheek. "All right, Professor Baldwin," he said huskily, "now that you've defined lust and gratitude for me, what about love? Surely you're not going to leave that out of your equation.''

She knew he wasn't taking her seriously but she didn't intend to stop now. "Love is a combination of those two plus esteem, consideration, devotion and veneration. It's not true that love is never having to say goodbye. Lovers are often separated, sometimes for a long time, but if they're truly in love that love will never die.''

Ethan sighed and caressed her back. "Oh, my little darling, I hope nobody ever pricks your balloon, but you have a highly romanticized way of looking at the world outside your own realm. Let's take our hot chocolate into the family room and talk. I'm intrigued by your hypothesis.''

He picked up one of the filled mugs and turned toward the family room.

"It's not a hypothesis," Brittany insisted as she reached for the other mug and followed him. "It's a fact.''

They settled themselves comfortably on the couch and sipped their hot chocolate. "Mmm, that tastes good," he said. "Maybe it will relax me enough that I can get a little sleep before morning.''

"I was having trouble dozing off when you called me," she confessed. "I couldn't get comfortable. It was almost like a premonition that something was wrong, but I don't believe in that sort of thing. I kept ignoring it until you called and I learned that something was wrong. Very wrong! Now I don't know what to think.''

"Maybe you should accept the fact that there are stranger things in this life than can be explained logically,'' he suggested.

She shook her head. "Why are you so willing to believe in ghosts and precognition when you won't believe in the power of love?''

He drank the rest of his chocolate milk and set the empty mug on the coffee table, then leaned forward with his arms on his thighs. "Probably because I haven't had any experience with ghosts or precognition, so it's not hard to accept the possibility of them, but I've experienced firsthand the hell love can wreak, and I'll never fall into that pit again.''

Chapter Five

Brittany was shocked by the bitterness in Ethan's tone. Was it directed at his ex-wife? Except for the day Hannah brought the baby over and announced that she was giving Ethan full custody of their son, he'd seldom mentioned her and then it was in conversation with his father, not Brittany. To the best of her knowledge he never discussed his marriage with anybody.

She put her hand on his back. "Ethan, I'm sorry you feel that way. It must make life awfully unhappy for you."

He straightened up and took her in his arms, then leaned them against the back of the sofa. "Bless you, my little darling." He hugged her and settled her head on his shoulder. "If anyone could make me believe in love it would be you, but I'm too old for conversions. The best I could offer you is great sex and reasonable financial security. You're way too young to even consider such a compromise."

"Just why do you think I couldn't make you happy?" she asked briskly.

"Because I wouldn't let you?" he answered truthfully. "I

fell 'in love' a long time ago with Hannah. We were so sure we were meant for each other that we married as soon as we finished college. Our so-called 'wedded bliss' barely survived the honeymoon before we discovered we had absolutely nothing in common. She was the high-powered 'make it to the top as fast as possible' type of person, whereas I was the casual, laid-back kind.''

Brittany liked the warmth of his arms around her, the stroke of his fingers through her hair and the occasional brush of his hand across her breasts. She nuzzled her face into the side of his throat and felt his muscles tense as his hand roamed below her waist and settled on her hip.

"Don't tease me with offers of warmth and comfort, Brittany," he warned her. "I have a very limited amount of self-control where you're concerned."

She rubbed her palm on his chest. His heart was racing in time with her own. "I'm not teasing you, Ethan. I just want you to know how good love can make you feel."

"And what makes you think that the feelings we're stirring up in each other is love?" he asked. "It could as easily be lust or gratitude. I know all about both of them. Don't forget, I was married for many years, and while my wife and I didn't like each other much we both had healthy libidos and no desire to play around. Our relationship was the same as any other married couple's. The only difference was that for us it was just having sex, not making love."

Brittany was uncomfortable discussing Ethan's intimate relationship with his ex-wife, but since he seemed to be willing there were some questions she'd like to ask.

"If you were so unhappy, why didn't you get divorced sooner?" she blurted, then felt the flush of embarrassment that rushed through her. "That is... I mean..."

"It's okay," he said as he rained kisses in her hair. "If I'm going to come on to you, you have a right to ask personal questions. For the first four or five years we really did try to make it work. Neither of us wanted to admit we'd been wrong. Also, Hannah's mother, Gerda, was devoutly religious and unalterably opposed to divorce. We were afraid she'd be devastated if we split up, and since she was in frail health, Hannah was reluctant to subject her to that.

"Finally, though, things got so bad between Hannah and me that we decided we could no longer live our lives to please another person. We filed for divorce but didn't tell Gerda, thinking she might not find out since she lived seventy-five miles away in Louisville and had little contact with the outside world."

"Unfortunately, we might as well have announced it in the newspapers." His tone was heavily sarcastic. "A so-called friend of Gerda's who lives here in Lexington and works at the courthouse saw the petition and mentioned it to her. Three days later my mother-in-law had a stroke from which she never recovered, although she lived for several more years."

"But that's not your fault," Brittany protested. "Especially if her health was bad, anyway."

"I know that, but I couldn't convince Hannah," he said. "She was so guilt-ridden that she insisted the petition for divorce be dropped and that her mother be brought to our house where we could look after her.

"Not that I minded taking care of her," he hastened to assure Brittany. "I was glad we were in a position to do so, but there was no more hope of divorce."

Brittany sighed. "It seems as if some people are just born to lead complicated lives. You lost your mother at an early age, then had an unhappy marriage as well as two unwell parents to care for—"

"No, Brittany," Ethan interrupted. "I've never thought of either Gerda or Nate as a burden. And don't forget, I have one blessing that blots out all the heartache. I have Danny. I wouldn't have had him if we'd divorced early in our marriage."

Something bothered her, and she decided that since he was sharing his story with her she'd ask him about it. "Ethan, do you mind if I ask just one more question?"

He smiled at her and tipped up her chin with his fingers. "I told you, you're entitled. What do you want to know?"

"Well, you told me once that you'd been divorced for two years," she said hesitantly, "but Danny is one and a half. If my arithmetic is right that means he was born six months or so after the divorce."

He nodded. "Your arithmetic is just fine, darlin'. We filed for divorce again almost immediately after Gerda died and didn't find out for a couple of months that Hannah was pregnant. She'd never wanted a family and it didn't make that much difference to me one way or the other, so Danny came as a real shock."

"I can imagine," Brittany murmured.

"Canceling the divorce again was out of the question," he continued. "We'd waited too long already to get on with our separate lives, so we finally agreed that since I knew absolutely nothing about caring for infants Hannah would keep the baby for the first two years and then I'd take him."

Ethan laughed. "In my blessed ignorance I expected that he'd get easier to handle as he got older. Nobody told me what little terrors they can be when they start to walk, and talk, and climb, and need to be potty-trained. Sheesh!"

Now it was Brittany's turn to laugh. "So now you can pity your poor mother. She had two of you the same age going through the same stage at the same time."

His arms tightened around her. "Yes, she did, and sometimes we tried her patience severely, but neither Pete nor I ever doubted her love for us. Just as I intend to see to it that Danny never doubts my love for him."

Brittany snuggled against Ethan. "You're such a good father. I don't understand how Danny's mother could just give him away like she did. Nobody would get a child of mine away from me.''

He nuzzled her temple. ''I don't doubt that, but don't be too hard on Hannah. At least she has the guts to admit that she's not good mother material. Not all women have your overabundance of maternal instinct, sweetheart.''

''I don't—'' she started to say, but he interrupted her.

''Maybe not an overabundance,'' he conceded, ''but you'll be a good mother when the time comes. Hannah isn't. She doesn't give Danny the tender loving care a child needs. She's too impatient, too resentful of the time his needs take her away from her work, but she didn't 'give Danny away.' She gave his father custody of him. She knew Nate and I would take good care of him. I was slated to have physical custody in six more months, anyway, and in the business world you can't always pick and choose your promotions. She makes a lot more money than I do, so she's going to pay me child support and set up a trust fund to assure our son's college expenses.''

Before Brittany could say anything the antique grandfather clock in the parlor started chiming. The resonate tones filled the air softly but then pealed only twice. Surprised, she pulled herself away from Ethan and stood. ''Oh, my gosh. It's two o'clock. I've got to go home or I'll never get up on time in the morning.''

Ethan stood also and looked at her. ''Why don't you stay here tonight. That's not a come-on. We have a couple of guest rooms, and that way you wouldn't have to wake up until Danny does. After all, it's my fault you're up so late.''

''Oh, I couldn't do that,'' she protested, although the invitation was almost irresistibly enticing. ''I...I don't have any night clothes.''

''I could loan you a pair of silk pajamas that my brother and his wife gave me one year for Christmas. They've never been out of the plastic sack. I don't wear that type of thing.''

She was seriously tempted. Imagine trying to sleep in his

pajamas with him just across the hall! Obviously that would be out of the question.

"I'm sorry, I really must go home," she said rather lamely, "but I'll be back on time in the morning. Don't worry."

"Well, if you insist," he agreed, "I'll walk you to your car."

She wasn't going to object to that even though it wasn't necessary. He put his arm around her waist and they walked side by side until they came to the driveway. Then he turned her to face him and put his other arm around her, too.

"I wish there was some way I could express my thanks to you for being there for me tonight when I needed you so badly." His tone was deep with emotion.

"You can show your appreciation by promising me that you'll never again hesitate to call on me if you need someone to stay with Nate and Danny after regular hours," she told him. "They are both special to me, and I'd never forgive you if you didn't ask me for help and something happened to one of them."

He rubbed his cheek against hers. "But they're not your responsibility, they're mine. I should have kept better track of Nate. He was more important than that damn meeting—"

"Stop beating yourself up over something you can't fix," she scolded affectionately. "Nate knows he has these memory lapses, and he remembered that you'd told him not to leave the room by himself. He has to share the blame for what happened. You know he wouldn't want it any other way."

"Yes, ma'am." She heard the merriment in Ethan's tone even though it was too dark to see his expression. "Any chance you could clear time to give me lessons on child care as well as home nursing?"

"No way," she said sternly. "The only thing you have to learn is not to lose your patience."

They both laughed at the unintended double entendre, but the chuckle quickly died as he lowered his head to meet her upturned face. Their mouths met and melded, and she snuggled against him as his tongue prodded her lips apart to gain entry.

Brittany felt as if she were floating into a cloud of ethereal sensations almost too exquisite to bear. She couldn't get enough of the way he nibbled on her lower lip and suckled on her throat, setting her blood on fire.

She wasn't prepared when he suddenly grasped her arms and stood her away from him. "Brittany, no, we mustn't do this!" he moaned, then turned from her and opened the car door. "Be careful driving home, and don't worry about getting here on time tomorrow. I'll wait for you."

Ethan watched until the car was out of sight, then went back in the house and put the pan and two mugs they'd used for the hot chocolate in the dishwasher. His hands shook so that he almost broke the mugs when they involuntarily banged together while he was holding them.

This couldn't go on! It was an impossible situation. It was bad enough that he lusted after Brittany so strongly, but knowing that she returned the feelings and, worse, thought those feelings were love made the whole predicament inconceivable.

He couldn't take advantage of those tender emotions! If she were older, more experienced, they could admit they were in the throes of passion and enjoy it while it lasted, but his starry-eyed young Cinderella expected a fairy godmother to bring her a Prince Charming who would love her forever.

Unfortunately he wasn't that man. He was a college professor with a small son and a sick dad, both of whom needed to be taken care of. It was foolish of him to have hired Brittany knowing about the magnetism between them, and now it was purely selfish of him to keep her on.

He'd break her heart if he did, and he'd break his own if he was forced to let her go.

He switched off the kitchen light and headed for the stairway. The most important thing he'd learned tonight was that he really needed a live-in nanny like Hannah had employed ever since Danny was born. He would prefer an older woman. One who had already raised her own children and didn't like living alone. A person like that would fit right in with his little family. She would help him raise Danny and also be a companion for Nate.

Actually, all his dad needed was someone to remind him to take his pills and his shots. He could give them to himself.

Ethan started up the stairs. But where was he going to find this paragon? Hannah never seemed to have much trouble finding help. Keeping it, yes. She was as difficult to work for as she was to be married to, but when one nanny left, Hannah always found another one without delay.

So why was he having such a time finding a permanent caregiver for his small son? Was he really searching as hard as he could?

Of course he was. It's true he'd had a few applicants to his want ad in the campus paper and turned them all down as unsuitable. After all, he couldn't leave his little boy with just anybody, although Nate was always here to make sure Danny was properly cared for. Still, "adequately cared for" wasn't enough. Babies needed a full-time mother, and Brittany was filling that role beautifully. She didn't just go through the motions, she even got down on the floor and played with Danny. He squealed with delight and grabbed handfuls of her beautiful shining hair when she blew raspberries on his bare tummy.

He'd never seen his child as buoyantly happy as he had been since Brittany started taking care of him!

And Nate. He couldn't love Brittany more if she were his own daughter. How could Ethan send her away when those two needed her so badly?

On the other hand, how could he not send her away when he knew it was not only folly but deceptive to let her stay.

How long could he hold out against his agonizing desire for her? Against the soft sweetness of her?

He reached the top of the stairs and headed for the master bedroom. Not very damn long, that's for sure, and if he gave in to his longing and seduced her, how could he ever live with himself? She'd expect a proposal, or at least a commitment, and in time the chilling coldness of a loveless marriage would start all over again.

No way! He wasn't going to let his hormones trap him into that pit a second time! Even more important, he wasn't going to let Brittany become a prisoner of her misconception of love.

Brittany fell asleep as soon as she crawled into bed, and the alarm woke her the next morning on time, feeling wide awake and refreshed. She'd fallen into the habit of having a light breakfast with Nate and Danny, so she left her apartment as soon as she was dressed.

Last night had been both terrifying and wonderful. The time they'd spent looking for Nate had been frightening, but the interlude after they found him and had him settled down had been pure bliss. How could Ethan insist that his own feelings for her weren't love when there was no way he could hide how much he wanted her?

He was right when he insisted a person could lust after someone without being in love with them, but she refused to believe that the tender way he treated her was lust. She knew all about lust. She'd been fighting amorous boys off ever since she was in her early teens, and they'd been nothing like Ethan. They'd been eager to score and didn't want to take the time to court her first.

Whereas Ethan held back, aroused but unwilling to act on that urge. Didn't that mean his feelings for her were deeper, more protective than just an itch to get into her knickers?

Of course he was older than any of the other fellows she'd dated, but he considered that a minus, not a plus. She wondered if he had any idea of the disrespectful, sometimes cruel way some young men treated their women. She'd learned early on to pick her boyfriends carefully.

She was five minutes late when she pulled up to the house. He must have been watching for her because he opened the door and strode toward her carrying his briefcase as she walked up to the porch. She smiled broadly, delighted to see him, but then noticed the frown on his face and assumed he was upset because of the time.

"I'm sorry, Ethan," she apologized, "I hit all the red lights on my way over here—"

"Brittany, we have to talk," he interrupted as if he hadn't even heard her. "Can you stay on for a while after I get home from school?"

"Well yes, of course," she said. "Do you need me to baby-sit?"

"We'll talk about it this afternoon," he told her, and started to walk past her but she stepped in front of him.

"Ethan, is something wrong? Nate? Danny?" She wasn't going to let him get away with putting her off. "I don't want to have to worry about this all day."

"Nate and Danny are fine," he assured her, "but I don't have time to go into what I want to discuss with you now."

This time he did walk around her. "See you later," he called, and hurried toward his car.

Brittany spent the rest of the day wondering what had happened between the time she left the house last night and the time she returned this morning. Last night they'd been burning for each other, but this morning he didn't even bother to say "hello." She couldn't honestly say his manner toward her was cold, but it had sure dropped into the chilly range.

At intervals she tried to worm some information out of Nate without actually asking him questions, but if he was aware of his son's mood he wasn't admitting it. He seemed oblivious to her efforts.

Two o'clock came and went with no sign of Ethan, but she hadn't really expected him to come home that early. Then three o'clock, the time he quite often appeared, but it wasn't unusual if he was later. By four o'clock she was having to restrain herself to keep from pacing the floor. She didn't want to upset Nate by letting him see how nervous she was, but every time an automobile came down the street and then drove on by she wanted to scream.

Finally, at twenty-one minutes to five she heard his car turn into the driveway and rushed to open the door. "Ethan," she called, and stepped out onto the porch. "Where have you been? I was afraid you were involved in an accident or something."

She sounded like a shrew, but she couldn't control herself. Now that she knew he was safe and had put her through all this anxiety for nothing, she was hopping mad. "If you were going to be late you should have called!"

He came around the car and walked toward her, a puzzled expression on his face. "I'm sorry, Brittany, I didn't know you'd worry."

She took a deep breath. No, of course he didn't. It was none of her business what time he came and went. He wasn't answerable to her. She was beginning to sound like Hannah.

"I—I'm sorry, too," she stammered. "I guess after that experience with Nate last night I'm a little skittish."

"You have a right to be," he said as he reached her and put one arm around her, but it was more a form of guidance than a caress.

When they got inside the house he released her and put his briefcase in the closet where he usually kept it. Danny spotted him and came running with his arms open, shouting "Da-da! Da-da!"

Ethan scooped him up in his arms, and father and son

played happily for several minutes while Brittany steamed. If Ethan didn't tell her what he wanted to talk to her about, and do it quickly, she was going to explode!

Then Nate appeared and he and Ethan went through the usual routine—"Hi. How are you? How was your day? How about that favorite baseball team?"—until Brittany finally put her hand on Ethan's arm and got his attention.

"Ethan, I hate to intrude, but you did tell me this morning that you wanted to talk to me this afternoon. If you don't mind I'd really like to get to that so I can go on home."

Ethan nodded and handed the baby to Nate. "Dad, would you mind putting him in his playpen? There are some things I need to discuss with Brittany. We'll be in the library if you need me."

Nate looked perplexed but took his grandson and said, "Sure thing, son. Take your time. Danny and I will get along just fine."

Ethan gestured to Brittany to precede him on their way to the library, and she became more mystified with every step. He'd never invited her into the library before, except for the time he'd been showing her through the house the day he hired her.

In fact, that was the last time she'd been in that room. Nobody had told her she shouldn't go in there, but he kept the door shut and she got the feeling that it was his private study.

Now he was not only inviting her in but making it plain by his demeanor that it was more of an order than an invitation. What had she done? Surely the fact she'd been a few minutes late wouldn't have perturbed him this much.

He opened the door and ushered her in, then closed it behind them. "Please, take a seat," he said, and waved her to the chair in front of the desk, then took the one behind it for himself.

She sank down, relieved to have something under her before her shaky knees gave way.

For a moment they just sat there, neither of them speaking or making eye contact. Brittany twisted her hands in her lap, and she noticed that Ethan had picked up a pen and was tapping it on the desk blotter.

Finally, he cleared his throat and looked at her. "Brittany…" His voice wavered and he cleared his throat again and started over. "Brittany, I don't know how to tell you this…" Again his voice broke and this time he took a deep breath before forging ahead.

Meanwhile Brittany was squirming and biting on her lower lip. *Get on with it,* she wanted to scream. *For God's sake, what's happened?*

"Ethan, just spit it out," she snapped. "Whatever it is it can't be as bad as most of the things I've been imagining today. What's happened? Is something wrong with Danny? Nate?"

She knew she'd already asked that and he'd said his son and his father were just fine, but what else could it be?

Was it possible something was wrong with his twin brother? But that wasn't something he'd hesitate to talk to her about. She didn't even know Peter.

"Brittany, I'm going to have to let you go."

She was so wrapped up in her tangled thoughts that her mind only processed part of what he said. "Go? Go where? I haven't asked for vacation time."

"No, you don't understand," he told her. "I—I'm trying to tell you that I won't be needing your services anymore."

She blinked and tried to make sense of what he was saying. "But of course you will," she protested. "After what happened last night—"

Then it hit her like a blow to the solar plexus, and she closed her eyes until she could catch her breath. "Ethan, are you telling me I'm being fired?"

She heard him draw a ragged sigh. "I wouldn't have put it that way, but yes, I guess I am. I've made other arrangements for the care of Nate and Danny."

Chapter Six

Brittany just stared at Ethan, unable to grasp what he said. He couldn't mean what she thought he did. Last night they'd been so close. He'd called on her for help in finding his father and she'd been happy to oblige. She'd come to think of Nate as the grandfather she'd lost, but her feelings for Ethan were anything but sisterly.

She hadn't made any secret of that, but could that be the problem? Had she come on to him too strong? She hadn't seen any reason to hide it. He seemed to be attracted to her, too.

She was jolted out of her trance by his voice. "Brittany, don't look like that. I'm sorry. I should have handled this more tactfully. Actually I've been wrestling with it ever since you left last night...."

"What did I do?" she wailed, still unable to make sense of what he was saying. "Is it because I was late this morning? You said last night—"

"Brittany, it has nothing to do with your work performance," he assured her. "You're wonderful with both Nate and Danny, but I feel it is time to move on. Your employment here was always meant to be temporary—"

"Oh, I see." She didn't see at all, but neither could she assimilate anything he was saying. She needed to get out of there and try to make some sense of what was happening. If she concluded that she was being unfairly treated she could argue with him about it later.

"I'll give you severance pay and excellent references...."

Now he was insulting her by putting their relationship on an employer-employee basis. She'd thought they had something much closer than that, but obviously she'd been wrong.

She stopped listening as she leaned over and picked her purse up off the floor beside her then rummaged through it for her keys. Without waiting for him to stop talking she stood up and started toward the door.

"Brittany!" he called. "Where are you going? I haven't finished yet."

She didn't bother to answer but opened the door just as he caught up with her. "Honey, I can't let you go like this," he said as he restrained her with his hand on her arm.

Still she said nothing. She couldn't even think let alone talk. Instead she jerked her arm out of his grasp and headed toward the front door with him at her side. "Look, I didn't mean to upset you like this," he said. "Please, don't rush off. Sit down and let me explain."

She reached her car and opened the door before he could stop her. "I need to let the agency know I'm available," she murmured, more to herself than to him. "Maybe they can put me to work tomorrow."

She slid behind the wheel, slammed the door shut and started the engine as Ethan continued to protest through the closed window. What was his problem? she thought. She'd been too shocked to catch much of what he'd been saying, but he'd put one thing across loud and clear. He didn't want her to work for him anymore!

Ethan watched impotently as Brittany pulled her car away from the curb, brakes squealing, and headed down the street.

Damn! How could he have screwed up so royally when all he'd wanted was to find a way to dismiss her without hurting her feelings or making her afraid her nursing and baby-sitting skills were somehow impaired.

He'd been up most of the night pacing the floor and even writing down what he wanted to say, but somehow it never sounded right. He'd driven around town for an hour after his last class at school today trying to make his mind work, but all he could call up was pain and angst at the thought of not having her here when he left for work in the mornings, and again when he came home in the afternoon.

He turned and walked back to the house. They hadn't been together a lot, he couldn't have resisted her sweet charm if they had been, but what little time they'd had was precious beyond belief to him.

Now what was he going to do? He'd let her go and had no one to replace her. Tomorrow was the last day of school and he'd get a substitute to handle his classes. Then there was a week's break until summer school started so he had ten days to find a full-time nanny.

When he stepped into the foyer he heard Nate playing with Danny in the family room. He couldn't face them right now so he detoured into the parlor and sat down. How was he going to tell them he'd fired their best friend in the whole world?

Nate adored Brittany. She'd done wonders for him and most of it wasn't even medical. He no longer had bouts of depression, or if he did they were much fewer and farther between. His diabetes was almost always under control now because she saw to it that he took his medicine and his meals on time, and she treated him like a loving grandfather instead of an obstinate patient.

And Danny. Danny had taken to her right away. She claimed to have little experience with babies, but she must have been doing something right. The kid would hardly let her out of his sight. A lot like his dad in that respect, Ethan thought grumpily.

There was going to be all hell to pay when those two found out she wouldn't be coming anymore!

Brittany headed her car for home and lost no time getting there. She knew she was in no condition to drive. It was almost like being on autopilot. She couldn't focus either her thoughts or her eyesight and was a danger to everyone on the streets.

One thought kept going round and round in her head. *What had she done wrong?* Everything seemed to be going so beautifully. She'd forgotten that the job was only temporary. Actually, she'd almost forgotten it was a job! That was her first mistake. She'd allowed herself to be drawn into Ethan's family, and it was nobody's fault but her own.

She'd been so happy, and she loved all of the Thorpe men, each in a different way but equally as strong. Obviously that love wasn't reciprocated. At least not by Ethan. He was the one who'd fired her, and that's what he'd done, no matter what he preferred to call it.

She'd thought Nate was fond of her, and she still thought he was, but not as deeply as she'd hoped. Ethan usually talked important decisions over with his dad, so they must have discussed this one, too, which meant Nate had agreed to it.

And what about Danny? Poor little guy, he didn't have any say in the matter. Instead, he'd be stuck with yet another stranger to get used to.

She knew Danny loved her and that he'd miss her. That thought wasn't a happy one considering that he'd already been abandoned by his mother and several nannies in his young life. Had Ethan found a permanent baby-sitter? He could at least have set her mind at ease on that score.

No! That wasn't fair. He probably would have if she'd stayed around to let him. He'd been trying to talk to her, but she couldn't stay there and listen. Even his words were garbled in her unregistering mind.

She pulled up in front of her apartment house and shut off the motor, but instead of getting out she crossed her arms on the steering wheel and buried her face in them. She knew she should get on the ball and start looking for another job, but she couldn't seem to function. She couldn't even cry. Although tears filled her eyes, she couldn't release them.

She needed to get in touch with her agency first thing in the morning. She couldn't afford to lose so much as a day's pay, even with the extra money Ethan was giving her for baby-sitting Danny as well as caring for Nate. Newly licensed medical assistants were at the low end of the wage scale until they had some experience, as were untrained child-care workers.

With effort she raised her head, opened the door and got out. She couldn't sit here in the street like a zombie for the rest of the day. So life had dealt her a painful blow. So what? She'd had them before and managed to survive. She'd get through this one, too.

Squaring her shoulders, she marched up the sidewalk to the front door.

A week later Brittany had just finished giving her last bed bath of the day and was packing up her equipment. The agency had put her to work as soon as she notified them that she was available, and now she was helping bedridden patients with bedside nursing so they could stay at home instead of in the hospital. She had several patients a day, but only spent an hour or two with each one.

She liked this arrangement better than having one patient full-time. This way she wouldn't become too attached to any one of them. She wasn't going to make that mistake again!

Saying goodbye, she left the house and got into her car. It was almost five o'clock and she was looking forward to a cooling shower and a hot fudge ice cream sundae sprinkled with salted peanuts. She didn't need anyone to tell her that was not exactly a proper dinner, but she'd dutifully bought herself a roast beef sandwich and a bowl of vegetable soup for lunch, so surely she was entitled to a treat tonight.

As she drove her unruly mind wandered to the Thorpe family. She hated it when that happened. She tried so hard to keep from thinking about them, but she couldn't help it. She worried about Nate, and about Danny. Were they all right? Did they miss her as much as she missed them?

And Ethan? Every time he popped into her mind, which was dozens of times a day, she made a determined effort to delete him, but it wasn't possible. The best she could do was think positively. Assume that he'd done what he felt was best for all of them, and make sure she harbored no bitterness.

As she turned the corner onto her street she saw the figure of a man sitting on her building's doorstep. He was too far away to identify clearly, but as she drew closer it looked like—Yes, it was. It was Nate!

He was wearing jeans, a pullover shirt and a baseball cap, and was just sitting there staring off into space. What was he doing here? And even more important, how had he gotten here?

She pulled slowly over to the curb and stopped. Did Ethan know his father was here? Getting out of the car she hurried up the sidewalk. "Nate," she called. "How long have you been waiting?"

He stood when he heard her voice and took off his cap. "Not long," he said. "One of the young ladies inside said you should be home soon so I just sat down to wait. I hope you don't mind."

Brittany threw her arms around him and hugged him. "Mind! I'm delighted, but how did you get here?"

He put his arms around her, too, and clung to her. "Why did you let Ethan send you away?" he asked without bothering to answer her question. "You didn't even say goodbye."

"I'm sorry about that," she said, "but I couldn't stay if Ethan didn't want me to and I was too upset to talk about it."

She belatedly realized they were making something of a public spectacle of themselves and pulled away slightly. "Look, we can't talk out here," she said. "Let's go up to my apartment and you can tell me what you're doing here. Does Ethan know you're gone?"

She took Nate's arm and led him upstairs to her studio apartment. "You sit over there," she said, pointing to the reclining chair, "and I'll get us a glass of iced tea. First, though, I have to ask again. Does Ethan know where you are?"

Nate shook his head as he sat down. "No. I waited until he left to take the baby to the doctor for his shots, then called a taxi and had the driver bring me here."

"But Ethan will be worried sick when he comes home and finds you gone," she remonstrated. "You remember how upset he was the night you wandered away from the meeting at the university."

"But I didn't wander away this time," he protested. "I left of my own free will."

Brittany opened her purse, took out her cell phone and handed it to Nate. "I'm not going to split hairs with you. Either you call Ethan or I will. You should be ashamed of yourself deliberately putting him through this kind of fear."

Nate ignored the phone. "He didn't give a thought to my feelings when he fired you."

She winced at the word *fired,* but Nate didn't notice. "Let him stew awhile. After all, you worked for me as well as for him. If he doesn't want you caring for Danny anymore that's his and Danny's loss, but it's my insurance money that pays my medical bills, and I'll damn well do the hiring and firing."

She knew this wasn't altogether true. No insurance company would pay for full-time medical care for a patient who was no sicker than Nate. He required supervision, not bedside nursing.

Nevertheless, she wasn't going to argue the point. It would

just upset him even more and make his blood sugar go down. Instead she punched Ethan's number herself. He answered almost immediately. "Please get off the phone," he barked. "I need to keep the line open—"

"Ethan, it's Brittany," she cut in. "Nate is here with me."

"Oh, thank God." It was a prayer of relief, not an exclamation. "I came home and he was gone. Where are you?"

"We're at my apartment. I found Nate sitting on my doorstep when I got home just now. He's okay—"

"I'll be right there," Ethan interrupted, and slammed down the phone.

Brittany turned hers off and put it back in her purse. "Now you've got him all upset," she said to Nate. "He's coming to get you."

"Won't do him any good," Nate said stubbornly. "I'm not goin' back."

"But why?" she wailed. "I can't believe that he's done anything to abuse you. He loves you dearly."

"He's got a fine way of showin' it," Nate grumbled. "He let you go, didn't he? And without even telling me. I just woke up one morning last week and you were gone. I even asked him if you'd quit and he admitted that he'd sent you away."

Nate looked down at his hands folded in his lap. "What kind of love is that? He didn't even ask my opinion or tell me he was gonna do it. I might have trouble remembering things, but I'm not stupid. I'm entitled to some say in my own life." He raised his hands and dropped his head in them.

Brittany sat down on the arm of the chair and put her arm around his shoulders. Apparently she was going to have to have a heart-to-heart talk with her favorite patient.

"Nate, listen to me," she began. "I can understand your frustration, but you have to admit that you need guidance."

He shook his head but she hugged him and continued. "Yes, you do. You have two medical conditions, diabetes and dementia. Both are controllable if you take care of yourself, but can be serious if you don't. At least give Ethan credit for caring enough about you to see to it that you get that supervision."

"I did give him credit," Nate protested. "I've never made any secret of how grateful I am to him for hiring you to be my nurse-companion. Of how much I depended on you."

Brittany thought about that for a few moments. "Could it be that was why he let me go? That he felt you were getting too dependent on me? I know he wants you to be independent for as long as possible."

"Even if that's true, it's no excuse," Nate stated flatly. "You were giving me the best possible care, but you weren't smothering me with it. He'll never find anyone better than you to look after me and Danny, and what's more he knows it. He's been ornery as a rodeo bull ever since you left. He's cranky, and impatient, and impossible to live with."

He raised his head and looked at her. "The last straw was last night when he told me he'd decided to hire a woman named Jessica Warren as a live-in nanny for Danny and caregiver for me. No way!" he exploded. "If he tries that I'll bring the baby and come over here and live with you."

Startled, Brittany opened her mouth to protest just as she heard footsteps pounding up the stairs and a knock on the door.

It was Ethan. "Brittany, are you there?"

"Come on in," she called. "The door's not locked."

Ethan opened it and strode into the room Brittany called an apartment. He located them both immediately, Nate sitting in the comfortable chair and Brittany perched on the arm with one of her arms across his shoulders. A bolt of jealousy tore through Ethan. He'd sell his soul to be the man she was caressing, but he quickly pushed that unworthy thought aside. Damned if he was going to be so petty as to be jealous of his own father!

Ethan was carrying Danny, and the minute the child spied

her he started to squirm and cried, "Ma-ma, Ma-ma." Brittany practically tumbled off the chair onto the floor and Danny wiggled loose from Ethan and waddled across the room, his little arms held out as he threw himself at Brittany and landed in her open arms.

They hugged and kissed and then Brittany began to cry. Not ladylike weeping, but huge, choking sobs that racked her whole body.

Ethan had to restrain himself from going to her. He'd never seen such an emotional reunion. Danny climbed all over her and kept repeating, "Ma-ma, Ma-ma," while they clung to each other as if they were afraid someone was going to separate them again.

But Danny wasn't even her child, Ethan pondered. Was it really possible that she could love another woman's baby as deeply as if he were her own?

Nate and Ethan just stood by and watched quietly until Brittany finally started to get herself under control and hiccuped as she rubbed one forearm across her streaming face. Ethan handed her his clean handkerchief, but before she could use it Danny put his little hands on her wet cheeks, wrinkled up his little face and said, "Ma-ma cry?"

By that time Nate was sniffling, too, and even Ethan had trouble holding back. There were times when he wished it was all right for men to cry, but he guessed someone had to keep his wits about him, and he'd had a lot of experience at that.

It was no wonder he had so much trouble keeping his relationship with Brittany in perspective. Apparently she was irresistible to all men from ages two to ninety-two and beyond.

Both Nate and Danny had been impossible ever since he'd let her go. Nate was able to articulate what was bothering him. He wanted his nurse back and he wasn't going to accept a substitute, but Danny was something else again. He'd been doing a lot of whining and calling for his "ma-ma," but Ethan had thought he meant Hannah.

Obviously he was wrong. When his son called for "Mama" he wanted Brittany. It must be true that just giving birth doesn't make a woman a mother. It takes emotional bonding as well.

However, Ethan was sure that Hannah wouldn't be pleased if she ever found out that Danny was calling Brittany "Mama." She may not want the bother of raising a child, but she was very possessive of anything she considered hers, and Brittany seemed to have cast some kind of spell over his whole family.

Ethan couldn't keep his gaze off Brittany. He'd never seen her so disheveled, nor so beautiful. Her glorious dark brown hair hung tousled and free from the center part to her shoulders. Mascara smeared her grass-green eyes and made little rivulets that trickled down her face.

He wanted to take her in his arms and hold her, tell her how much he'd missed her, how badly he wanted her, but if he did that he wouldn't be able to stop until he'd made commitments he didn't want to make. It wasn't fair to any of them to start something he couldn't, wouldn't finish.

Oh, he could make love to her, all right. Right here on the floor if he didn't keep a tight rein on his control, but good sex wasn't enough and they both knew it.

She was wearing a wrinkled white lab coat over green scrubs, which must mean she was working. A feeling of loss flooded over him. Well, what had he expected? Of course she was working. Anyone as skilled and as compassionate as she would be in great demand in the medical field.

He sighed. If only she were older and he less jaded!

Finally, when Brittany had wiped her face and everyone had calmed down a reasonable amount, Ethan turned to Nate and said, "Are you satisfied, Dad, now that you've managed to get all of us riled up?"

Ethan realized that was unfair as soon as he'd said it, but he was still wrung out from all the emotionalizing that had been going on ever since he'd arrived home and found Nate not there.

"It wouldn't have been necessary if you hadn't treated me like an idiot child," Nate shot back.

Brittany, who was still sitting cross-legged on the floor with Danny in her lap, spoke up. "All right, you two, enough of that. We'll never get anywhere if you can't be civil to each other."

Ethan, who was sitting on the edge of the bed, nodded. "You're right. I apologize, Dad, but you scare the hell out of me when you take off like that. Why didn't you come to me and tell me what was bothering you?"

"I did," Nate insisted. "You wouldn't pay any attention to me. Just kept saying we didn't need a medical assistant anymore, we needed a nanny-housekeeper. Brittany can do that, whatever it is. She'd be a great nanny, and anybody can keep house.

"As long as I've got your attention, though, I'll tell you one thing I won't do. I won't agree to letting that Warren woman live in my house."

"But why?" Ethan asked, exasperation thick in his tone. "What did she do to you?"

"She didn't do anything to me," Nate admitted, "but she doesn't like kids and I'm not gonna let you hire her to take care of my grandchild."

Ethan had almost reached the end of his rope. What was Nate talking about? Jessica Warren had seemed to be the motherly type, and she was certainly experienced after raising four children of her own.

"Why do you say she doesn't like kids?" he asked. "You only saw her for less than an hour the day she came to the house for an interview. It seemed to me she was very efficient."

"As a housekeeper, yes," Nate agreed, "but Danny was cross that day, remember?"

Ethan thought back and remembered that his son had been pretty cranky. He'd whined and pulled at Ethan to be held, but nineteen-month-old children frequently had bad days.

"I remember, but—"

"Well, do you also remember that you got an important phone call in the middle of the interview and you put Danny in the playpen in the family room and took the call in the library?"

"Yes. So?" Ethan asked impatiently.

"Danny didn't like being left behind, and he tuned up full volume and howled in earnest," Nate said. "I was in the breakfast room and headed toward the family room to see what was the matter. When I got there she was standing at the playpen with her back to me shouting at the baby."

Ethan was shocked. This was the first time Nate had mentioned this episode!

Before Ethan could ask questions Nate continued. "I can even tell you exactly what she said. She said, "Shut up, you spoiled brat! What you need is a whole lot of discipline and I'll see to it you get that once you're in my charge.""

Ethan was appalled. Was this the truth or was his dad making it up? He'd never known Nate to lie to him before, but could he be hallucinating?

No, Ethan wouldn't even consider that. If Nate said it happened then it happened. He wasn't hallucinatory! Still, he had some explaining to do.

"Why didn't you tell me this before?" Ethan asked.

Nate shrugged. "I wasn't sure you'd believe me. She was puttin' on a real good show for you, braggin' about her little grandchildren and tellin' you how much she loved them. To tell you the truth, I thought you had better sense than to hire her. I could tell the minute she came in the door she was a phony. I've seen her type before."

Ethan didn't know whether to laugh or cry, figuratively speaking, of course. Now that it had been pointed out to him, he could see that Nate was right, wily Ms. Warren had managed to put something over on him.

Oh, he would have caught it once she started living with them, but then he'd have to start all over again in his search for a nanny, not to mention the damage the woman might have done to Danny's little psyche in the meantime.

He sighed and admitted defeat. "Okay, Dad, I admit I was too eager to find a sitter and not careful enough about whom I chose, but you have some explaining to do, too. We'll discuss that later, but now, do you trust me to ask Brittany to come back and work for us without messing it up, or do you prefer to do it?"

Ethan saw the ghost of a smile on Nate's lips. "You're the one who fired her so you owe her an apology. Just try not to screw it up and drive her further away."

Ethan laughed. All of a sudden he felt good. No, make that *great*. It was as if a heavy black cloud had been lifted, letting the sunshine in. He'd missed Brittany to the very depth of his being but hadn't been able to admit it. Not even to himself. Instead he'd blamed his foul mood on the weather, Nate and Danny's equally foul moods, and his unrewarding search for domestic help.

Now, if he was extremely lucky and didn't botch everything again, he was going to get her back. He might even consider admitting to himself that he was hopelessly in love with her, but that would take a lot more soul-searching. He'd thought he was in love with Hannah and he'd served years in purgatory for his mistake in judgment.

He wasn't going through that again, but he and Brittany could get to know each other and see how things worked out.

Ethan walked across the room and hunkered down in front of Brittany and Danny. She had a wary look in those tear-drenched eyes, and he felt like a bully for making her cry like that.

He reached out and took one of her hands in his. "Brittany…"

His throat was raspy and he cleared it and started again. "Brittany, if I give you my firstborn will you come and live with us full-time?"

She hesitated, and for a moment he was afraid she was going to refuse but then she smiled. "Will you toss in Nate, too?"

She'd been teasing him! "Done," he said quickly.

Nate tried hard to look insulted. "Well hell, you could have thought it over a few minutes before giving me away." His eyes danced with glee.

"I was afraid she'd change her mind," he explained with a chuckle.

Turning his attention to Brittany, he said, "Now that we've got that straightened out we'll have to discuss your salary and what your duties will be. Why don't you come home with us? We'll have dinner and talk about it."

She looked as if she might be going to refuse, and he quickly reached out and poked his son's round little belly with his finger, making the child giggle. "Besides, I don't want to set this one off again by trying to take him away from you."

That seemed to be the right answer. She laughed and squeezed the little guy. "Well, if you're going to put it like that, how can I refuse? First, though, I've got to take a quick shower and get into some clean clothes. You all go on ahead and I'll catch up with you shortly."

Ethan would have agreed to anything to see her beautiful face light up the way it had now.

Ethan and Nate left, and Brittany gathered up clothes and towels and made her way to the bathroom at the end of the hall that was shared by all six tenants in the four upstairs studio apartments. She locked the door and undressed as she ran hot water for her shower.

Her hands still trembled, and she felt as if she'd been run through a wringer. She was both embarrassed and ashamed at the way she'd broken down when Danny ran to her calling her "Ma-ma." She hadn't cried in the week since Ethan had fired her but had obviously been storing up all that grief inside. When it finally broke loose it was a deluge.

Nate and his family had caught her completely off guard and she was still trying to adjust. What she couldn't figure out was what did the Thorpe men want of her? Nate needed a nurse, Danny needed a nanny, and Ethan apparently needed a housekeeper-mediator.

The three jobs together sounded suspiciously like the duties of a wife, except that Ethan had made it plain that another wife was the last thing he wanted.

She picked up her dirty clothes and stuffed them in the plastic bag she'd brought, then stepped under the shower. Ooo-oh, that felt good! The water ran off her hair and was blessedly cool on her overheated skin. Her shampoo and body gel were the same fragrance and when she closed her eyes she could see fields of colorful wildflowers.

She suspected that Ethan didn't really want her at all but had been coerced into taking her back by his dad and his baby son. She wasn't enthusiastic about returning under those conditions, but she couldn't let Nate and Danny down.

There was one thing she was sure of, though. If she went back to work for Ethan there would be no more hanky-panky! Not that she knew exactly what that term implied. It had been her grandfather's phrase, but she suspected it meant "making out."

On second thought, she wasn't sure she knew exactly what that meant, either. Was it just "fooling around" or did it include sex?

Well, whatever, there wasn't going to be any of it if she moved into Ethan's house!

She turned off the shower and patted herself dry with her thick towel, then stepped out of the shower stall and hurriedly dressed in the clean forest-green shorts and T-shirt she'd brought to the bathroom with her. It was one of her newer outfits and—

Oh, darn! What was the matter with her? These shorts and shirt were special favorites of hers because everyone told her how nice she looked in them. How the green brought out the matching green of her eyes.

She raised her head and looked at herself in the medicine cabinet mirror. She didn't want to seem self-centered, but the colors did flatter her. Subconsciously, without meaning to, she'd dressed in a "come-on" fashion for Ethan. Here she'd just resolved not to flirt with him and all the time she was dressing to please him, up to and including the short shorts!

Well, there was nothing she could do about it now. She was all dressed and ready to leave. Her hair was still wet but she didn't want to take the time to blow-dry it. Danny had cried and held out his arms to her when Ethan had taken him from her. She didn't want to upset him any more than he already was. Her hair would dry fast enough once she got out in the hot Kentucky sun.

All the way to the Thorpe residence her mind was in turmoil. Was this a mistake? She'd already faced the fact that she was in love with Ethan, and that the rest of his family had stolen her heart. She wanted to spend her life with them. She wanted to give Ethan more children.

That was all fine and good, but he'd been equally blunt in letting her know that he was not and never would be in love with her. Or anyone else ever again, although if she were older he wouldn't mind having an affair with her.

So there she was tied up in semantics again. Just what did "affair" mean? If she remembered her high school French correctly, *affaire de coeur* meant "affair of the heart." She didn't hear marriage mentioned anywhere in there. In popular fiction it seemed to indicate "shacking up together." She knew what that meant and wanted no part of it!

How could she ever meet an eligible man she could love and who would love her if she spent all her time at the Thorpe's taking care of them and mooning over her unreciprocated love for Ethan?

The attraction between them was too strong. Before long they'd be involved in an affair no matter what the definition, and she did not want to live her life on the thin edge of respectability, unwilling to have children because their father wouldn't acknowledge them by giving them his legal name.

There was one way she could walk that thin line. She'd have to behave like the employee she was, and not like the potential wife she'd like to be. She could mother Danny to her heart's content because he needed mothering and there was no one else to do it.

She could be a doting granddaughter to Nate because he needed the nursing care she was trained to give and enjoyed being coddled, but Ethan was strictly off limits. He neither needed nor wanted anything from her except the services he would be paying her to minister to his father and little son.

He'd just have to keep his libido under control!

Chapter Seven

Brittany settled back into life with the Thorpe men without a hitch. She loved living with them, and although she was supposed to have weekends off, she seldom left the house. On Ethan's advice she'd given up her apartment. He was right, there was no reason to pay rent on it when there was plenty of room for her seven days a week in his big home. He was very scrupulous about not asking her to do any work on Saturdays and Sundays, but she always pitched in and volunteered when she saw a need.

She loved being part of a family. Although her mom and dad had loved her and she'd felt the same way about them, there had been no real closeness between her and her parents. There'd been no room in their lives for a child. She'd been raised by disinterested hired help much the same as Danny would be if Hannah hadn't relinquished custody of him to Ethan.

The sensual tension between Brittany and Ethan had abated somewhat and they were both more relaxed. Brittany attributed this to her rigid resolve to keep her distance from him both physically and emotionally. It wasn't easy. In fact it was darn hard, especially when she caught him looking at her with that perplexed look in his expressive eyes after she'd chilled him out when he touched her or said something a little too personal to her, but it seemed to be paying off.

She'd learned that he could play that game, too, so they kept their conversations light and their touching nonexistent. It wasn't as difficult as she'd expected since he usually shut himself up in the library in the evenings to read or work on lesson plans.

She and Nate played with Danny until his bedtime, at which time Nate usually retired, too, leaving Brittany to watch television or read as she chose.

It was a tenuous situation at best. So many times she wanted to touch Ethan, caress him, say something a little intimate that would make him grin and return the intimacy, but she didn't dare. She was convinced that kind of behavior had been what prompted him to dismiss her before. He didn't want her love. He didn't even want her affection. He just wanted her to keep his father and his son happy and that's what she was doing.

They seemed content, but she was restless. By mid-June the weather was hot and steamy, and although the house was air-conditioned, the atmosphere was heavy and oppressive.

Sometimes she loaded Nate and Danny in her car and took them to one of the malls. They were always downright chilly and crowded with people shopping or just wandering around enjoying the free entertainment.

One Saturday at the end of June when Ethan had taken Nate and gone over to Louisville to do some fishing in the Ohio River, she took Danny and went to Victorian Square, a re-stored block of nineteenth-century buildings featuring a collection of retail and specialty stores.

She was pushing Danny around in his stroller, stopping now and then to admire the arrangement of merchandise in a window, when she heard someone call her name. She turned and blinked at the handsome dark-haired man coming up behind her.

For a moment she was perplexed, then it came to her. It was Colin McTavish! He'd been one of her group of friends the year she spent at the university. "Colin," she said with a broad smile. "I didn't recognize you at first. You've grown a beard."

He chuckled. "And I wasn't sure it was you. Is this yours?" He gestured toward Danny. "Is he why we don't see you around school anymore?"

She laughed. "No, Danny's not mine. I'm his nanny. I work for his father."

Colin leaned down and chucked the baby under his chin. "Hi, guy," he said, then straightened up. "He sure is a cute little fellow," he commented, "but how are you? I'm so sorry about your parents. I was studying in France last summer and didn't hear about the accident until I got back. By then you'd moved and everybody had lost track of you."

She nodded. "Yes, I'm sorry." She went on to tell him about her deceased parents' bankruptcy and the fact that it had been necessary to drop out of the university and enroll in the abbreviated medical assistant's course so she could support herself.

"That's a real bummer," Colin said, "but all the more reason for you to stay in touch with your friends. We would at least have given you the emotional support you needed."

She patted his arm. "I know that now, but at the time I just didn't want to see or talk to anyone."

Danny began to chatter and pound on his stroller. Colin reached down and ruffled the child's hair. "You okay, fella?" he asked, then turned to Brittany. "Why don't we keep walking? We can talk while he enjoys the motion."

"Fine," she agreed, and started pushing the stroller slowly.

Colin told her about his summer in France and that he'd just completed his second year at the university. He bought the three of them ice cream cones and they sat down on a fancy wrought-iron bench to eat them. Brittany had asked for a plastic spoon and used it to dish strawberry ice cream into Danny's eagerly opened mouth.

Colin watched for a while then shook his head. "I can't get over you working as a nanny for Professor Thorpe's kid."

"Why?" she asked. "Do you know the professor?"

"You better believe I do," Colin said grimly. "I gather you didn't take one of his classes the year you were in school?"

"Well no, I didn't," she admitted.

"Then take my advice and don't. If you need to pass an English class in order to graduate, find someone else's. This guy will flunk you if he possibly can."

Brittany was shocked. Not the sweet, kind Professor Thorpe she knew. "I find that hard to believe."

Colin shrugged. "I'll have to admit I'm exaggerating, but I guarantee if you survive one of his classes you're going to know everything there is to know about the English language."

She giggled. "Is that so bad? It seems to me we could use more teachers like him."

Colin used his paper napkin to wipe ice cream off Danny's mouth and chin. "You are a messy kid, do you know that?" he chided the child good-naturedly while Danny opened his mouth and looked pleadingly at Brittany for more.

She laughed and shoveled another spoonful into it. "Just one of the joys of being a nanny."

They watched in silence for a while as the people went by until he spoke. "Hey, look, you don't work all the time, do you?"

She shook her head. "I have weekends off if that's what you mean."

"Yeah, that's what I mean. There's going to be a concert at the university next Saturday night called Beer and Ballet. It's casual dress and high-class entertainment being put on by the music department. Some of us will be getting together afterward for beer and pizza. I've got an extra ticket if you'd like to go with me.''

Brittany automatically opened her mouth to refuse but then closed it again. Wait a minute. She was entitled to Saturdays and Sundays off, holidays, too, but still she felt guilty even thinking about accepting Colin's invitation.

Could it be because going out with another man felt too much like being disloyal to Ethan?

But that was just plain ridiculous! He'd never shown any interest in asking her for a date, so how could it matter to him one way or the other if she started seeing other men?

No, her feelings of guilt no doubt stemmed from her recent bereavement. It's true she hadn't been dating since her parents' deaths, but that had been a year ago. It was time for her to get out, meet new people and have a little fun.

Besides, how could she ever get over her ill-advised love for Ethan if she never met other men?

She cleared her throat. "I'd love to go with you, Colin.''

After discussing what time he'd pick her up the following Saturday, Brittany and Colin parted and she headed home. Although it was almost six o'clock in the evening, the hot Kentucky sun shone brightly, and she was surprised to see Ethan's car in the driveway. She hadn't expected them to get back from Louisville for another couple of hours.

She got out of the car and had reached into the back to get Danny out of his car seat when the front door opened and Ethan came out. "Let me get him,'' he called as he hurried toward her. "He's too heavy for you to wrestle in and out of that seat.''

She momentarily bristled at his assumption that she was too weak to manage a squirming toddler, but then she remembered that Danny really was almost too heavy for her to heft out of tight places. She did it all the time when Ethan wasn't there, but if he wanted to play the gallant rescuer, who was she to object?

"Aren't you and Nate home a little early?" she asked as he reached in and tugged Danny out of the car.

"A little," Ethan confirmed, "but the heat over in Louisville is even muggier than it is here. I didn't want to take a chance on Dad getting heat stroke. Besides, the fishing was lousy."

"Sorry to hear that," she commiserated. "Danny and I went over to Victorian Square and had a great time. He loved being pushed around in his stroller and I met up with a friend I used to run around with the year I was in college."

"That's nice," Ethan said as they entered the blessedly cool house and closed the door on the heat outside. "Don't hesitate to invite her over here anytime you want to."

"Thank you, I will," she said, "but it's not a 'her,' it's a 'him' and he's taking me to the Beer and Ballet concert next Saturday night. I told him to pick me up here."

Ethan had been bent over putting Danny down on the floor, but now he straightened to his full height and glared at her. "You're going out with a man!" It was more of an exclamation than a question.

Brittany's eyes widened. "Well, yes. Do you have something against dating?" What was the matter with him? He looked like she'd hit him.

He didn't answer her question but came at her with a barrage of his own. "Who is he? What do you know about him? Where is he from? How come you haven't mentioned him before? Why—"

She finally caught her breath and held up her hand. "Whoa. Slow down. I'm not asking your permission to go out with him," she informed Ethan firmly. "I don't ask about your dates."

"I don't have dates," he growled.

"Well, that's your problem, not mine," she said loftily, and followed Danny in his wobbly rush to get to his grandpa, who was watching television in the family room.

The atmosphere in the house for the rest of the evening was decidedly cool. Ethan and Brittany spoke only when necessary, and although Nate didn't ask questions he could see that something was wrong and tried to keep the conversation going and lighten up the mood.

Brittany was perplexed. It was obvious that Ethan didn't want her to go out with Colin, but why? She and Colin had dated casually for a year before they lost track of each other, and she knew he was born and raised in Lexington, well brought up and studying to be a civil engineer.

There was absolutely no reason for Ethan to object to their friendship.

Ethan felt as if he'd been betrayed. Like a man who'd just found out his wife was cheating on him. But Brittany wasn't his wife, and she certainly wasn't cheating on him. He had no right to expect her to remain celibate since he wasn't willing to take the vows that would bind them.

But dammit, he was responsible for her! She was living in his home, caring for his father and his child, and she was so heartbreakingly young. Didn't that entitle him to make sure she wasn't doing anything foolish?

But what was foolish nowadays? So many of the moral codes had fallen by the wayside. If she were his daughter...but she wasn't his daughter and the feelings he had for her were definitely not paternal.

Things had been going along fairly smoothly since she moved in with them, although he was never sure just what her feelings for him were. Before he'd made the stupid mistake of firing her, she'd seemed as eager for him as he was for her, and he'd been the one who had to put the brakes on. However, since she'd come back she'd been sweet and loving with Nate and Danny but cool and distant with him.

He'd taken the cue from her and kept his passion for her under control, but it was a constant battle with himself not to storm down the barriers and melt that icy surface.

Brittany finished bathing Danny, rocked him for a few minutes while she sang one of his favorite lullabies, and put him in his crib.

In one of the few short conversations she and Ethan had had since she'd told him about her date with Colin, Ethan had asked her to come to the library after she got Danny to bed. What did he want? Was he going to harangue her again about her date? If he did it would probably mean she'd have to look for another job, because if he didn't fire her she'd have to quit. There wasn't anything she wouldn't do for Ethan if he *asked* her nicely, but she wouldn't let any man *tell* her what she could and couldn't do.

When she was sure Danny was settled she went downstairs and knocked on the library door. Ethan's voice answered immediately. "Come in."

She opened the door and he stood from where he'd been sitting behind his desk. "You don't need to knock, Brittany," he told her softly. "Every room in this house is open to you."

Relief washed over her. Apparently he wasn't going to scold her! "Thank you," she murmured, then realized she'd used up her whole vocabulary for the moment.

"Please, sit down." He gestured toward the chair in front of the desk then sat again behind it.

There was a short, uncomfortable interval of silence until Ethan broke it. "I...I want to apologize to you. I was way out of line earlier and I'm deeply sorry."

She gasped. This wasn't what she'd expected. She was glad he'd come to understand that he had no right to boss her around, but she needed to clear up a few rules. "I accept your apology, Ethan. I probably shouldn't have been so quick to take offense, but you caught me by surprise. I still don't know why you were so upset.''

"Don't you?" It was almost a whisper. "No, I suppose you don't.'' He shook his head and raised his voice. "It's just that I'd never heard you mention a boyfriend before, and when you—"

"Colin isn't my 'boyfriend,'" she informed him. "There were a group of us living on campus who were friends. We ran around together, dated each other, that sort of thing. When I didn't go back to the university after my parents died I just sort of drifted away from them...." Her sentence trailed off as her thoughts wandered.

"Anyway, I was really glad to see Colin this afternoon," she continued, "and when he invited me to go to the concert with him I said yes. I'm of age, Ethan. There was no reason for me to ask your permission.''

Ethan looked away. "You're right, but if you wanted to go why didn't you tell me? I would have taken you.''

Brittany couldn't believe what she was hearing. "You would?''

He nodded. "Does that surprise you? It shouldn't. What man wouldn't be proud to escort you anywhere?" He paused. "On the other hand, why should you go out with me when you can have your pick of all the handsome young men on campus.''

She didn't know what to say. Why was he paying her all these compliments now when usually he hardly noticed her? She was afraid of responding for fear of saying the wrong thing.

The magnetism between them was radiating enough heat to cause a meltdown. If she did what she wanted to do she'd go behind that desk, put her arms around him and snuggle up to his warm, muscular body, but being too forward is what got her into trouble with him in the first place. If she deliberately tempted him again he'd probably fire her, and she wasn't going to be that unsubtle. This time if he wanted her the first move would be up to him.

She pushed her chair back and stood. "I'm sorry for the misunderstanding," she said as he stood, too. "I assure you I know Colin McTavish well and he's a very nice guy. If you're here next Saturday when he picks me up, I'll introduce you. You might remember him. He says he's taken one of your classes."

Ethan looked interested. "Oh, which one?"

She grinned. "I don't know, but he said that anyone who passes one of your classes will be well versed in the English language."

He cocked one eyebrow. "Was that a compliment or an insult?"

Her grin turned to a chuckle. "A little of both, I think. He indicated you are a hard taskmaster."

"Well, he's got that right," Ethan admitted. "I can't be bothered wasting my time trying to teach students who have no desire to learn."

They had somehow moved closer together than was advisable, but Brittany couldn't make her legs take a step back. "Are you going to give me a bad time when I go back to school to study for my degree?"

He brought up both hands and cupped her face. His palms were soft and smooth on her cheeks, and she watched, mesmerized, as he lowered his head until she could feel his fresh breath on her mouth. "You'll never be in one of my classes," he murmured. "I wouldn't allow it. You're far too distracting."

He leaned down and kissed her on the lips ever so lightly, then quickly let her go. "Now, get out of here," he said brusquely, "and don't forget I want to talk to McTavish before he takes you anywhere."

Brittany didn't get much sleep that night. Every time she closed her eyes she saw Ethan's suntanned face slowly descending to her upraised one until their mouths touched. It had been so gentle as to be almost innocent, but there was nothing virginal about it—the ardor that motivated it was intense and passionate. However, by the next day, he was back to his friendly employer-employee mode as if last night had never happened.

Maybe it hadn't, she told herself. Maybe she'd just dreamed it all.

For the following week Brittany made an effort to keep her thoughts off Ethan and skipping ahead to the Beer and Ballet concert at the university theater. Named for its unique blend of the classical and the redneck, it was an annual event that had been going on for several years, but she'd never attended one of the performances before.

As the end of the week approached, Ethan started to get grumpy again. He complained about things that had never bothered him before, and even fussed at Danny for behavior all little ones engage in now and then.

Brittany didn't know what was the matter with her employer but she was getting pretty tired of it.

By the time Saturday rolled around he was in a real snit, starting at breakfast when he discovered they were out of his favorite cereal and continuing all day until, after Danny's nap, she took him to one of the parks that had a playground for children in order to escape.

Danny enjoyed playing on the small-scale, brightly colored slides and swings until a glance at her wristwatch told her it was time for her to start getting ready for the concert.

Ethan met her at the front door when they got home and took Danny from her. "Isn't it getting a little late?" he asked. "What time does that concert start?"

"Not until eight," she told him. "Colin is going to pick me up here at seven-thirty, so I've got plenty of time to get ready. Don't forget it's casual dress."

She walked toward the stairway and Ethan headed toward the kitchen with Danny in his arms.

An hour later Brittany had showered, shampooed and blow-dried her hair, and was dressed in white jeans, a sleeveless red banana-print shirt and ankle-high boots. Her face was innocent of makeup since this shimmering heat tended to melt even oil-free undercoat and mascara.

With a steady hand she outlined her full lips with liner, then filled them in with lipstick the same color as her blouse. A close inspection in the mirror assured her she'd made a wise choice, and she dropped the tube of lipstick in the small clutch bag she planned to take with her tonight.

She was standing on the landing at the top of the stairs when the doorbell rang. ''I'll get it,'' she called.

That would be Colin, and she hoped Ethan would take the hint and let her have a few minutes to chat with her date before interrogating him.

No such luck. Ethan was striding to the door before she even reached the first step. All she could do was hope he would be a gracious host and not treat Colin as if he were here to take an overprotective father's virgin daughter on her first date!

She hurried down the stairs as the two men shook hands, and Colin was the first to see her. ''Hi, honey,'' he greeted as she approached. ''You look gorgeous, as usual.'' He put his arm around her and hugged her.

It was just a friendly squeeze, but she saw Ethan scowl and her own temper began to rise. ''Thank you, sir,'' she said lightly. ''And you are still the best-looking man I know.''

That wasn't true. Oh, he was handsome enough even in the blue jeans and denim shirt he was wearing, but not as much so as Ethan. She just said it to let Ethan know he wasn't the only man she was attracted to.

Ethan's expression didn't change, and Brittany felt ashamed

of herself for taunting him. After all, he was just looking out for her.

"I won't offer you a drink since you'll be driving," he said to Colin, "but I would like to talk to you for a few minutes if you have the time."

Brittany felt a wave of dread, but Colin seemed pleased. "I'm early, and as you know you're only a mile or so from the university so we have plenty of time."

"Good," Ethan said, and led them into the parlor. "Please sit down. There are just a few things I'd like to ask you.

"Brittany tells me you took one of my classes a couple of years ago?"

Colin's face flushed, and she knew he was wondering if she'd told Ethan what Colin had said about him and his teaching methods.

"Yes, sir, I did," he said, then actually laughed. "I never studied so hard in my life, and still I only got a B."

Brittany relaxed with relief. Now she remembered something she'd forgotten about Colin. He was never intimidated by anyone. Not even the college professor he called "sir."

Ethan laughed, too. "I didn't remember your name when Brittany told me about you, but I recognized you as soon as I saw you just now. You were the brightest kid in that class, but you tended to malinger. That's why I piled the work on you. You could handle more than the other students and I wasn't going to let you waste all that intelligence."

Colin glowed with pride. "Thank you, sir. You taught me not only to assimilate facts but also the shortcuts on *how* to do it. In case you don't remember, I'm studying to be a civil engineer and now I'm getting straight A's."

"Good for you," Ethan said as he glanced at the grandfather clock and stood up.

"I didn't mean to keep you so long," he apologized. "I'd hate for you to be late for the concert."

Colin and Brittany jumped up, too, and Colin put out his hand. "It was a real pleasure to meet you again, Professor."

Ethan took the proffered hand. "Same here, and call me Ethan."

He let loose of Colin's hand and walked to the door with them, but when Brittany and Colin stepped out onto the porch Ethan spoke again. "Uh...Colin, Brittany has become pretty special to the Thorpe family since she's been working for us, and I guess we're a little protective of her since she has no parents of her own...."

His voice trailed off and Brittany felt the hot blush of part anger and part embarrassment. Damn him! She knew he'd pull something like this!

"What I'm trying to say," he continued, "is that I feel responsible for her, so take it easy on the drinking. If you need a ride home just call me and I'll come and get you."

"Ethan!" she muttered through her teeth. "You have no right—"

Colin put his hand at her elbow. "It's all right, Brittany." He looked at Ethan. "If it comes to that I'll bring her home in a cab, Ethan, but thanks for the offer."

Ethan watched as they got in a nearly new white Toyota and drove off. Damn! He'd done exactly what he'd promised himself he wouldn't do. He'd acted like the father of a teenager on her first date. He'd seen the anger in Brittany's expression before Colin intervened and led her away, but he couldn't help it.

He hated the idea of her drinking even though she was old enough, and the prospect of Colin drinking and then driving with her in the car was terrifying.

If anything happened to her... The notion was unbearable! It was also a case of overreacting.

From what he remembered of Colin McTavish from a couple of years ago, he was a bright and responsible young man who always had his work in on time and was serious about his goals. If he drank to excess it had never been brought to Ethan's attention by drunken behavior or hangovers in class.

Ethan went back into the house and headed for the family room. It was time to put Danny to bed, and after that he'd catch up on his reading.

The chimes in the grandfather clock struck twelve just as Ethan finished his novel, and he closed the book and turned on the television. Might as well watch the news until Brittany came home, which should be any time now. Those concerts seldom lasted more than three hours.

Actually, she could easily have been home before this, but they probably stopped somewhere for a drink. He tried to talk himself out of that thought. There was beer on sale at the concert, so why would they need to stop at a bar for more liquor?

His attention had been so exclusively diverted to Brittany that he didn't hear the first few minutes of the news until an announcement flashed on the screen that read News Break and a voice broke in.

We've just been informed that there's been a two-car collision at the intersection of Euclid and Main. No details as yet but stay tuned. We'll bring them to you as they come in.

A shiver of apprehension froze Ethan. That wasn't far from the university! Could it be some of the concertgoers who were involved? He sat down before his shaking knees gave way.

Get a grip on yourself, man, he told himself. Even if it was someone from the audience, hundreds of people would have attended that function. It would be too much of a coincidence if Brittany and Colin were involved.

It seemed like an eternity, although it was probably no more than ten minutes at the most, before the next news break came on.

We've been informed there are two fatalities in that auto-

*mobile collision we reported earlier, but so far the victims
have not been identified. However we do know that one of the
cars is a white Toyota and the other a blue Ford. Stay tuned—*

Ethan didn't hear the rest. The car Colin McTavish had been
driving tonight was a white Toyota!

Chapter Eight

Brittany was having a great time. She'd forgotten how much fun it could be to hang out with the gang, go to concerts, sports events, or just sit around and talk.

Tonight she'd covered all three bases. The concert had been a hoot with the audience dressed in shorts, slacks or jeans and seated at round tables on the floor. They were served their choice of beer or soft drinks while they watched the music department's excellent interpretation of the classical ballet *Romeo and Juliet.*

She and Colin had met the rest of their friends there and afterward had gathered for pizza and partying at the home of one of the fellows whose parents were out of town. It was a big house with a game room that contained a pool table as well as a floor suitable for dancing on and a CD player with wraparound sound.

Brittany was having so much fun that she lost track of time until during a lull in the music and the conversation she heard a clock chime. The student sitting next to her on the floor looked at his watch, then jumped up and exclaimed, "Holy

Moses, I'm sorry to break up the party, guys, but I've got a summer job and if I'm even a little late I'll get fired. I've got to go home and catch a few Zs.''

Brittany hadn't counted the number of times the clock chimed but now she looked at her watch and found that it was three o'clock. She could hardly believe the evening had gone by so fast!

She'd never had a deadline for when she was supposed to be home from a date. Her parents were seldom around, and the various nannies and housekeepers who took care of her in their absence hadn't bothered to argue with her about it.

In this case, though, she felt a little uneasy. Ethan went to bed at around eleven o'clock and she was usually sacked out before that. Surely he wouldn't wait up for her. No, of course not. She was a full-grown woman and could stay out as long as she wanted to.

Even so, the party was over. Everyone was standing up and Colin came over and offered her his hands. She took them and he pulled her to her feet and into his arms.

''Are you ready to go?'' he asked.

''Yes,'' she said. ''It's been a wonderful evening. Thank you for bringing me.''

''My pleasure. Thanks for coming with me.'' He gave her a squeeze, then released her.

It was close to four o'clock before Colin pulled his car up in front of Ethan's home and turned to look at Brittany. ''Is the professor apt to be upset about you coming in so late?''

She'd been wondering that, too, and hoping he'd been asleep for hours. ''Ethan?'' she blustered. ''Oh, no. What I do on my days off is none of his business.''

They got out of the car and Colin walked her up to the porch. The lights were on but he put his arms around her and was just lowering his head to give her a good-night kiss when the door was wrenched open and Ethan stood there looking like death warmed over.

"Where in hell have you been?" he demanded.

She was too surprised to do anything but gasp. He truly looked ill. His complexion was gray, his hair tousled as though he'd been running his fingers through it, and his brown eyes, usually so bright and shimmering with flecks of gold, had lost all their luster and were lifeless and desolate.

She felt Colin stiffen beside her. "Now, look, chum…" he growled, but Brittany put her hand on his arm in hopes of reassuring him until she could find out what had happened to unnerve Ethan so badly.

Her knees quivered and she could hardly speak. "Ethan. What's the matter? Is it Nate?"

Then another possibility shook her. "Oh, God, surely not Danny!"

Ethan shook his head and reached for her. "I thought you were dead!" he moaned, and his whole body trembled as he hugged her close and buried his face in her hair.

Brittany was vaguely aware of Colin walking past them through the open doorway and into the house as she wound her arms around Ethan's neck and caressed his back.

After a while he spoke again. "I've been going out of my mind," he said raggedly. "Why didn't you phone me and let me know you were all right?"

She nuzzled his neck. "Darling, I haven't the faintest idea what you're talking about—"

Just then Colin came toward them from the kitchen with a whiskey decanter and several glasses on a tray. He took them to the parlor, then came back and put his hands on Ethan's shoulders. "Come on, fella," he said as he gently pulled Ethan away from Brittany and headed him toward the parlor. "Let's get you set down before you fall down. You've obviously had a nasty shock. I've raided your liquor cabinet. A few belts of your best whiskey should help to steady you."

They walked into the room with Brittany right behind them, puzzled and without a clue.

Colin set Ethan on the sofa, and he leaned over and put his head in his hands. Colin poured whiskey from the crystal decanter into a bar glass and handed it to Ethan.

"Here, drink some of this," he said firmly. "You need something to calm you down."

That's for sure, Brittany thought as she watched him take the glass. His hand shook so badly that the whiskey nearly spilled. She sat down beside him as he took a large swallow that made him cough, then another before putting the glass down on the antique coffee table and reaching for Brittany. She was aware that Colin was watching them with a guarded expression, but for now it didn't matter. She'd sort things out with him later. Now her big concern was for Ethan.

She snuggled into his embrace, but it was Colin who spoke. He paced slowly in front of them as he directed his remarks to Ethan. "I need to know why you thought Brittany was dead, then I'll leave. I don't want to pry into your personal affairs, but you're not exactly making sense and I have to know she'll be all right alone with you."

Ethan's arms tightened around her. "Didn't you hear about the accident?"

Both Colin and Brittany blinked. "What accident?" they asked in chorus.

Ethan took a deep, stabilizing breath and told them about the news breaks that had been coming over the television. "At first I was concerned simply because it was pretty late and I'd expected you home earlier, but then when they showed pictures of the accident scene in which the fatalities had occurred I was terrified. The car was an exact replica of yours, Colin, and it was totally crushed."

He rubbed his cheek in Brittany's hair again. "That's when I began going out of my mind," he told them. "I called the police, the highway patrol, the sheriff, but the victims hadn't been identified yet. Still haven't been. I considered waking Nate and Danny and taking them with me to go down there, but the officers I talked to were adamant in their objections. They said there were too many people blocking traffic already and it was no place to bring a child or an elderly person with medical problems.''

Brittany shivered and Ethan kissed her on the temple. "I'm sorry, sweetheart. I shouldn't be telling you this, but now maybe you can understand why I behaved like a maniac when I opened the door and saw you standing on the porch.''

She raised her head. "But you seemed more angry than relieved.''

"I guess I was,'' he admitted. "Frankly, I couldn't handle all the emotions that roared through me with the subtly of a freight train.''

He started counting on his fingers. "There was the lingering terror that I felt when I thought you might be dead, relief that you weren't, and fury that you hadn't called to let me know you were safe.''

"But I—''

"I understand,'' he interrupted. "You didn't even know there'd been an accident, but who said I was making sense by then?''

Colin stopped his pacing and looked at Brittany. "Will you be okay?''

She nodded and sat up straight, disengaging herself from Ethan's embrace. "Yes, we'll both be fine. It was just a misunderstanding....''

"Well, then I'll be leaving.'' He turned toward the foyer.

Brittany stood and joined him. "Thanks again for everything,'' she said as they walked to the door. "I'm sorry—''

Colin reached for her hand and squeezed it. "Don't apologize. I just hope my parents didn't see the same newscast and are worrying about me.''

She opened the door and he stepped outside. "I'll call you in a few days if that's all right.''

"Please do,'' she said with a smile.

Ethan was no longer in the parlor when she walked in, but she noticed a light on in the family room at the end of the hall. She picked up the tray of drinks and carried it with her. As she neared the room she heard the CD player playing softly and noticed that the lamps had been turned on low.

What was going on here? Ethan didn't usually play romantic music or arrange dreamy settings. In fact, he avoided that sort of thing when they were together.

She went through the large entry and saw him sitting on the sofa facing the fireplace. There was no fire, it was too hot to light one, but the huge stone fireplace was a focal point of natural beauty.

She walked over and stood in front of him. He looked up, turned slightly so that he was sitting at an angle between the back and the arm of the sofa, and held up his arms. She set the tray on the coffee table and sank down beside him.

He cradled her across his lap. "I need you," he murmured in her ear. "I need to hold you, touch you, kiss you. I need to know you're here, safe in my arms."

"I'm sorry you got such a scare—" she started to say before he interrupted.

"You had no way of knowing about the accident, and I shouldn't have jumped to conclusions so quickly." He ran his hand up the outside of her jeans-clad thigh.

She caught her breath and tightened her arms around his neck. Their faces were on the same level, and unable to resist she brought her lips to his, hesitantly but insistent. She heard the rumble of a moan deep in his throat as he opened his mouth in welcome.

She wasn't sure what to do next, but he took over and taught her tongue to dance. Her heart pounded in an erotic rhythm as his hand continued its journey upward across her hip then stopped.

Brittany squirmed with the unfamiliar throbbing at the core of her being and pulled Ethan's shirttails out of his pants, then gasped as he cupped her breast in his hand, sending hot blood surging through her veins.

She slipped her hand under his shirt and caressed his bare back, stopping now and then to draw lines and circles on his skin with her fingernails. It made him shiver and buck against her derriere.

When they reluctantly pulled apart she buried her face in the side of his neck and labored to catch her breath.

"My goodness!" was all she could think of to say as his awkward fingers struggled with the small buttons on her blouse. "Oh, my goodness."

His fingers stilled. "Do you mind?"

Mind! How could she mind? She'd never been so revved up before in her whole life.

"No, please don't stop," she begged as she gently sucked on his earlobe.

"I don't think I could even if I wanted to," he murmured. "You know this is madness, don't you?"

She blew in his ear. "I don't care. I want you so much. I never intended to stay a virgin all my life. Just until the right man came along…"

Too late she realized he'd stopped unbuttoning her shirt.

He growled a barnyard expletive and set her off his lap.

Oh, damn! Now she'd done it! How could she have been so stupid. He'd told her early on that he wasn't going to make love with her because she was a virgin, but she'd hoped that in the heat of passion he'd forget that resolve until they'd actually done it. After that the point would be moot.

Now that happy event would probably never happen!

She watched his expression change from loving to uncertain.

He stood. "You knew I didn't intend to have sex with you since you were inexperienced, didn't you?"

Now that it was too late she found herself incapable of

telling him anything but the truth. She bit her lower lip and said, "Yes, I did."

"Then why were you coming on to me so strong?" he growled. "Why didn't you stop me? Were you deliberately seducing me?"

Looking down at the floor, she nodded. "Yes, I was," she confessed, then looked up and into his eyes. "I'm an adult. I have a right to make my own choices, Ethan. I also have a right to make my own mistakes."

He shook his head. "That's true, but you're forgetting one thing. Your rights end where mine begin. I have an equal right not to make love with any woman I might be attracted to but don't find suitable...."

"Suitable!" she exclaimed. "What does that mean?"

"You know what it means," he told her. "We've been over it many times. You're too young for me to have intimate relations with. I could get fired from my teaching job and lose custody of my child, to name just a few of the consequences."

He ran both hands through his hair. "I can't deal with this tonight," he said hoarsely. "Go to bed and we'll talk about it in the morning."

She hated to leave things the way they were now and made an effort to talk. "Ethan—"

"I said we'd discuss it in the morning," he said flatly. "Now, go to bed!"

She did.

Ethan poured more whiskey in a glass as he watched Brittany stride up the hall to the foyer and the stairway. What kind of idiot was he, anyway? Had he suddenly lost his mind? Why was he blaming her for his mistakes?

He was supposedly the mature one in this romantic soap opera. She was little more than a child. How could he expect her to play his adult games? It wasn't difficult for a single man to get his male urges satisfied in this sophisticated society where almost anything goes. But if he were an honorable bachelor he'd choose a woman of his own age, experience and ultimate goals.

He didn't doubt that she thought she was in love with him. She'd probably thought she was in love with Colin when she was going with him, too. There would be other men in her life before she settled down to be a wife and mother, but he wasn't going to be one of them.

He had a father and a baby son to take care of. He wasn't going to add a teenage wife to the list. At least, she wasn't far out of her teens. So what was he going to do about her?

There wasn't going to be a repeat of what happened tonight, that was for sure. And since he found her so totally irresistible he was going to have to send her away. Just the thought made his heart shrivel with pain.

How could she have insinuated herself into his very being in such a short time? And with him fighting it all the way? It didn't make sense! He'd only known her a few weeks and already she was the very essence of his heart and soul.

The clock struck six and he finished off the whiskey in his glass. Thank God it was Sunday and he didn't have to go to school. Instead he was going to bed and try to get some sleep. He didn't want to think about what would happen the next time he confronted Brittany.

Brittany had had a bottle of beer at the concert and another one at the party afterward. Not much, but even so, it was enough to relax her and put her to sleep once she crawled into bed.

She seldom drank anything alcoholic at all but sometimes took just enough to be sociable, and that's what she'd done last night. After that scene with Ethan she hadn't expected to sleep at all, but here it was ten o'clock in the morning and she barely remembered falling into bed.

She stretched and yawned. Ethan was in charge of Nate and

Danny on the weekends, so she could take her time about getting dressed and going downstairs.

She wasn't looking forward to facing Ethan. She knew he was angry with her for tempting him the way she had, and he had a right to be. What she'd done was unforgivable. How could she ever expect him to take her seriously if she behaved like an oversexed enchantress?

She sat up and swung her feet onto the floor. She'd made a mistake, but was it really so terrible? Yes, it probably was since he'd be the one doing the deflowering, but if she was willing to sleep with him, why should he care whether she'd had a lot of lovers or none at all?

After all, it didn't matter to her that he'd been married for years, and she was pretty sure he hadn't been celibate for the two years since his divorce, so why was he making such a big deal of her virginity?

She loved him and wanted to be with him, preferably married, but what was so great about a piece of legal paper that was easily revocable? There was almost one divorce for every two marriages in this country. He could always get out of it later if he wanted to.

That thought depressed her, but as she dressed she shook off the blues. If she ever managed to bring this stubborn man to the altar she'd make him so happy he'd never want to leave her.

His feeling for her might be just lust like he said, but she loved him enough for both of them.

Ethan was sitting at the breakfast table with a cup of coffee and reading the newspaper when Brittany walked in. He didn't glance up and she didn't know whether to greet him or not. He didn't look as if he were in the mood for cheery conversation, but they had to talk and the sooner the better.

"Good morning," she said blithely as she crossed the small

room and poured herself a cup of coffee. "Do you mind if I sit with you?"

"Mornin'" he mumbled behind the paper. "Sit wherever you want to."

Well, that wasn't exactly a warm welcome, but maybe she could heat it up. "Did you get any sleep last night?"

"No," he said, then folded the paper and put it on the table beside him. "Did you?"

He looked as if he hadn't slept in a week. His eyes were bloodshot and there were lines of fatigue around his mouth. She felt like a traitor for having gotten four hours of uninterrupted rest. After all, she was the reason he'd been awake all night.

"I...um, well yes, I did," she confessed. "I slept very well. I guess it was the beer that relaxed me—"

He shook his head. "You don't owe me an explanation. You're entitled to have a good time and stay out as late as you please."

She felt her lower lip quiver. "But I don't want you to be mad at me."

His features relaxed and his tone softened. "I'm not mad at you, Brittany. I'm angry with myself. I shouldn't have carried on the way I did over the minuscule chance you were involved in that accident. I'm not your guardian, and I'm sure not your father. I had no right to assume either role."

She felt all squiggly inside. "But I appreciate you worrying about me. Not many people have done that before. I was pretty much raised to take care of myself. I'm sorry I put you through such torment last night, but—"

"No, Brittany," he interrupted. "I don't want to hear you say you're sorry again."

He picked up his paper and stood. "When you've finished your brunch I'd like to talk to you in the library. Take your time. No hurry."

He walked away, leaving her with an empty stomach and no appetite.

Half an hour later, after she'd checked on Nate and Danny, who were watching a Disney movie on television, she took a deep breath and knocked on the door of the library. Ethan called for her to come in, and when she did he reminded her that he'd told her it wasn't necessary for her to knock.

She took the client chair he indicated and he slumped down in his chair behind the desk.

Taking off his glasses, he rubbed his eyes and said tiredly, "I'm afraid we have a real problem, Brittany."

She'd known one of them was going to have to bring up this subject and she wanted to be the first. "Ethan, if it's about last night—"

He nodded. "Yes, it's about last night, but don't blame yourself. I accept full responsibility and I'm deeply ashamed that I lost control the way I did."

She blinked. "But I thought... that is, you..."

"I had the effrontery to blame you for my transgression," he said, finishing for her although that wasn't exactly the way she'd intended to say it.

"Ethan, you're not entitled to all the blame," she told him. "If you remember, I wasn't exactly resisting. In fact, I was more eager than you were."

She stood up and walked to the window, then stood there with her back to him. "Also, you'll notice that the only thing I'm apologizing for is putting you through so much anguish when you thought I was in that car accident. I have no intention of apologizing for making out on the couch with you. I enjoyed it too much to regret it."

She heard him slide his chair back. "This is exactly why older men have no business romancing much younger women," he said. "You don't know what you'd be missing if I tied you to me at such an early age."

She heard him pacing the floor behind her. "From what

you've told me, I gather you've had a fairly unfettered up-bringing. You've been allowed to do as you please, when you please, with few restrictions."

She tried to agree but he continued. "Last night is a good example. It never occurred to you that I might worry, even if there hadn't been an accident, when you didn't come home until four o'clock in the morning."

Again she tried to interrupt and again he stopped her. "I'm not blaming you, I'm just pointing out the difference a generation can make in viewpoint. You behaved like the liberated young woman you are who is of age and on her own, and I acted like the father who has nourished and protected you and now finds it hard to let go. Neither of us is wrong, but neither of us is right, either."

Brittany seethed with frustration as she turned around to face him. "Dammit, Ethan, you're not my father!"

He glared back at her. "I'm only too well aware of that!" he said grimly. "And that's why this arrangement is impossible."

Fear clutched at her heart. "Wh-what does that mean?" she asked shakily.

"It means I'm going to have to send you away again." His expression and his tone were burdened with sadness. "And this time it will be for good."

Brittany's eyes widened and she sank down in her chair. "But...but why? I promise not to stay out so late again without letting you know I'm all right—"

Ethan sat down heavily into his chair behind the desk. "You still don't understand," he said dolefully. "I can't live with you in the same house and not come on to you. You're too beautiful, too sexy, and there's too much magnetism between us."

"But that's what I'm trying to tell you, Ethan," she said eagerly. "We've talked about this before but it bears repeating. I know you don't want to get married again, but there isn't any reason why we can't just live together, is there? Last night I met with a lot of the friends I hadn't seen for a year and most of them have live-in arrangements.''

She noticed that Ethan looked as though she'd proposed they set off an atomic bomb or something, and hurried on before he could stop her.

"Now, don't say anything until you've thought about it," she urged. "Why should we waste all those lovely feelings we have for each other just because your first marriage was a miserable one? We've got a perfect setup. I'm already living here as a nanny. Nobody needs to know our sleeping arrangements.''

"Oh, hell," Ethan groaned as he ran the fingers of one hand through his hair. "If the only impediment was my unhappy experience with marriage, I'd marry you as soon as possible, but that's not it. It's your age, Brittany. How can I make you understand. You're too young for me!''

She breathed a huge sigh of regret. There was no way she'd ever get Ethan to change his mind. She might as well give up and accept the inevitable. He wanted her gone and there was nothing she could do but leave.

Oh, she could put up a fuss, get Nate and Danny on her side and make life so miserable for him that he'd finally give in and let her stay, maybe even marry her, but he'd never forgive her. And she'd never forgive herself!

A relationship, whether marriage or cohabitation, needed mutual love and trust in order to survive, and a forced relationship could never have either of those. If she seduced him beyond his control and they made love, he'd marry her. She was pretty sure he'd even insist on it, but it would be a bleak union.

Ethan's voice cut through her musing. "Brittany, are you all right?"

Her body jerked slightly. "What? Oh, yes. I'm fine. Umm…when do you want me to leave?''

He looked surprised, as if he'd expected more of an argument. He probably had from past experience, but this time she just wasn't up to it.

"As soon as you can find another job and a place to live," he said.

She fought with herself not to ask the next question, but she had to. It was too important to her to know the answer. "And what about Nate and Danny? Do you have another nanny-cum-nursemaid lined up to care for them?"

Her tone sounded sarcastic, but she truly hadn't meant it that way.

He winced. "You know I don't. I just decided I'd have to let you go a few hours ago. If worse comes to worst I'll cancel the classes I've scheduled to teach this summer and look after them myself while I search for more permanent help."

She rose heavily from the chair, all of a sudden feeling ninety-one instead of twenty-one. "Well, you can start looking immediately, because it won't take me long to find both a new job and an apartment. The college kids from out of town are going back home for the summer, which opens up both housing and employment here in Lexington."

She turned and walked toward the door. "For that matter, I'll go call my nursing agency right now. They can probably put me to work soon. They're always short of—"

"No!" She had her hand on the knob when his voice rumbled across the room. "That is, I...I didn't mean you had to leave immediately. I'm not throwing you out, for heaven's sake...."

She turned to face him and he was standing behind his desk. If she didn't know better, she'd think he looked as confused as she knew she did.

Ethan was as surprised as Brittany was by his outburst. She was doing exactly what he'd hoped she'd do, making it easy for him to get rid of her, and he couldn't bear to let her go.

If she walked out that door she'd take his heart with her, and everybody knows you can't live without a heart.

Surely she could put off leaving for a little while. He hadn't envisioned her moving away within hours, or even days. If he'd given it any thought, he'd assumed it would be weeks at the soonest.

Now he was standing here with his objection noted, his mouth open and nothing coherent to say.

Chapter Nine

"There...there's no reason to put it off," Brittany suggested sensibly. "I have to work, and I need a place to live. Besides, I want to get resettled as quickly as possible. The longer I stick around here, the more attached I'll become to Nate and Danny, and it's going to be much too painful leaving them as it is."

Ethan noticed she hadn't included him in those she'd miss. Well, what had he expected? She wasn't preparing to leave of her own volition, he was sending her away.

But it was all for her own good, he told himself as he had so often before. One of these days soon she'd meet a personable young man her own age, get married and start a family.

That thought was excruciating, and he turned his face away so she couldn't see the pain mirrored on it!

"You're welcome to come and visit us...uh...them," he told her.

"No, that would only prolong the agony of separation," she said. "Let's get this over with as soon as possible. Have you told Nate yet?"

Ethan shook his head. "No, and that's another thing I want to talk to you about. Please, come back and sit down." He indicated the chair she'd just left.

For a minute he was afraid she was going to refuse, but then she walked slowly toward him and reseated herself. She crossed her long, slender legs, which were bare clear to the bottom of her short little royal-blue skort. Everything had been happening so fast since she'd entered the room, and he'd been so dreading the confrontation they were going to be having, that she'd come across as a beautiful blue whirl, but now he was aware of every inch of her shapely figure, classic features and rich dark brown hair that swung free to her shoulders.

It was a pleasure just to look at her, but he couldn't sit here all day gazing. Folding his hands on the desk he tried to gather his thoughts about him enough to make a simple request.

He cleared his throat. "Brittany, would you mind doing me a favor? I know I have no right to ask, but...well...I need your help with Dad."

Immediately her expression was filled with concern. "Nate? What's wrong with him? I've made sure he's been taking his injections—"

"No, no," Ethan assured her. "It's not his health, but you know the way he reacted the last time I sent you away."

She looked as if she were going to object, but he hurried on. "Dad was always a caring father to Pete and me even before our mother died, and I have an immense amount of respect for him, but he's got a stubborn streak a mile wide."

Ethan squirmed in his seat. "Frankly, I don't know how to deal with it. I was wondering if...well...if you'd tell him you're leaving because you've been offered a better job. You know, more money, better benefits—"

He realized even before he'd finished the sentence that he'd made a big mistake.

"In other words, you want me to lie to him," she accused as she stood up. "Make him think I don't care about his and

Danny's welfare as long as someone else is waving the almighty dollar in my face—''

He jumped out of his chair, too. "No, that's not what I'm saying," he interrupted. "Please, Brittany, sit back down and hear me out. I'm obviously doing this badly, but I haven't had any sleep for over twenty-four hours and my brain is scrambled. Just let me try to make you understand."

They both sat back down and Ethan ran his hands over his face. "I shouldn't have tried to handle this until after I'd had a nap, but I knew if I kept putting it off I'd never do it."

Her expression softened and she reached across the desk and put her hand on top of his. He turned his over and clasped hers, then raised it to his lips and kissed it. "This is very painful for me," he rasped.

She closed her eyes for a moment, but then shook her head and withdrew her hand from his. "Yeah, tell me about it," she said sarcastically.

"I'm sorry you feel that way," he said. "You certainly don't owe me any sympathy, but I really do want what's best for all four of us. That includes not upsetting Dad any more than is necessary. You know what that does to his overall health."

She settled back in her chair and nodded. "Yes, I do know, and I agree with you. I'm sorry for acting like such a shrew, but I'm afraid neither of us is at our best right now."

He managed a tired smile. "You could never act like a shrew. I only wish I had your patience and understanding."

She sighed. "Well, now that we've established this mutual admiration society, I've got work to do."

She stood and again headed for the door. "I'm pretty sure the agency will be able to place me in another position soon. You'd better make arrangements for Nate and Danny as soon as possible. Meanwhile I'll try to think of a way to tell Nate I'm leaving without upsetting him too badly."

She reached the door and looked back. "I'll spend the rest

of today looking for an apartment, so I'll probably be able to move out of here sometime in the next few days.''

She opened the door and left.

Brittany stumbled out of the library just in time. No way was she going to let Ethan see how badly he could hurt her ever again. She was through crying over him. She didn't know what he wanted of her, and for that matter neither did he. He drew her close with one hand and pushed her away with the other.

She knew he didn't mean to torment her, but that's what he was doing with his waffling. Actually, if he hadn't fired her again she'd have quit. Just not quite so abruptly.

Her medical agency was available twenty-four hours a day so the first thing she did was call them. They were delighted to hear from her and told her they'd have an opening within a couple of weeks. That was okay with her since she still had to find an apartment and tell Nate she was leaving.

She walked across the hall to the kitchen and filled two thick mugs with coffee and set them on a tray, added a plate of sugarless cookies that Nate had made the day before, and carried the tray to the family room. He was sitting on the sofa facing the television, and when he saw her he picked up the remote control and shut the set off.

"Well, good morning," he said cheerfully. "I was beginning to wonder if an elf had come in the night and carried you off. Do you know it's nearly noon, girl? That must have been some party you went to last night."

She sat down beside him and handed him one of the mugs. Apparently he didn't remember greeting her not more than forty-five minutes earlier when she'd first come downstairs.

She hated it when he had a bad-memory day. Sometimes it came back, but other times it didn't. Such as the time he wandered away from the university and got lost. Would a different caregiver give him the close attention he needed? She couldn't bear to think of him getting lost and terrified again.

"You got that right," she told him lightly, determined not to let him know about the most recent lapse in his memory. He was pretty good about handling those things on his own if he later remembered them, but if they had to be pointed out to him and he still couldn't remember it frightened him.

She knew he hadn't heard any of the turmoil that had erupted down here last night. He was slightly hard of hearing, and he'd been asleep in his room upstairs. The house was nearly soundproof and he removed his hearing aid when he went to bed.

She took a sip of her coffee and set the mug back down on the coffee table. She had a difficult task to perform and she might as well get to it.

"Nate, I have something to tell you," she began.

He scowled. "Do you have to? I've found that when a person starts a sentence like that it almost always turns out to be something I don't want to hear."

Brittany clenched her fists in her lap. Damn Ethan. Nate was his dad, not hers. Ethan was also a college professor, eminently more qualified to counsel people and handle difficult situations than she, but still he couldn't admit to his father that he'd fired one of the household help.

She cleared her throat. "Oh, I don't think you'll mind hearing this. Actually, it's good news." She almost choked on that last sentence.

"I...I've been offered another job." She felt Nate stiffen as he turned his head and glared at her.

"You're not going to take it, are you?"

She looked away, unable to face him as she deliberately misled him. "Well, yes, I am. It pays more money and has better benefits."

For a moment there was a strained silence, then Nate asked, "And what about Danny? Who's going to look after him? I guess I can take care of myself okay, but who's going to look after Danny while Ethan's teaching?''

She felt a sob rising in her throat and fought to hold it back. ''That's Ethan's problem.''

She sounded callous, but it was grief rather than uncaring. ''Believe me, Nate, I'm not as unfeeling as it must seem to you, but I have to take care of myself as well as my patients. In order to make a living in my field I have to take advantage of every opportunity.''

She sniffled. ''You must know how much I love you and Danny, but I can't afford to pass up this assignment. I have only myself to rely on, whereas you know that Ethan will take good care of you and his little son.''

''He'd take good care of you, too, if you'd let him,'' Nate muttered.

Brittany turned to stare at him, unable to believe what she'd heard. ''I beg your pardon?''

''Oh, can't you see the man's crazy about you?'' Nate growled. ''Even I can see that and half the time I don't even know what day it is.''

It hurt her to hear him put himself down. ''Don't talk about yourself like that,'' she scolded. ''It's too easy to slide into a depression if you don't keep a cheerful attitude. You're doing just fine and you know it, so quit trying to be a matchmaker and behave yourself.'' She finished on a more upbeat note.

He fixed a stern eye on her. ''And are you going to try to make me believe you don't have feelings for my son?''

She felt her face flush but hoped it wasn't too noticeable. ''Of course I have feelings for him,'' she blustered. ''He's sweet and kind and I'm very fond of him—''

''Oh, come off it, Brittany,'' Nate grumbled. ''Sweet. Kind. Fond of him. You and Ethan seem to think I'm an imbecile. Hell, I was young once. For that matter I'm still not over the hill, so why are you two sidestepping and sashaying around the issue? Why don't you admit that you're in love with each other and get married. That would solve all our problems.''

Brittany was stunned. She'd been sure Nate was unaware of the electricity that flowed so freely between Ethan and herself, and here he'd known about it all the time. It was embarrassing and also a little maddening.

"I don't see where that's any of your business," she said loftily.

"It is when it deprives me of the medical care I need," he shot back.

"You're not being deprived—" she started to argue.

"The hell I'm not," he roared. "If you leave it will deprive me of the excellent care you've been giving me."

How could she argue with a man like that? His memory might not be all that great but he had a sharp mind. He knew how to get his own way. But then so did his son, and when the two strong-willed men got on a collision course, who knows what could happen?

"Now you're being ridiculous," she told him. "You do a fine job of looking after yourself, and with a little supervision you're able to take care of Danny, too. My main job lately has been acting as his nanny, and originally that wasn't even in my job description."

Nate set his mug back on the tray. "Tell me, Brittany, did you actively seek this new position?"

"Yes, I did," she said, happy he'd asked a question she could answer without being evasive.

"Was that before or after Ethan fired you?" Nate asked innocently.

"After," she answered just before she realized she'd stepped into a booby trap.

"That's what I thought!" he chortled.

"Dammit, Nate, that's not what I meant!" she protested vigorously. "Besides, you have no right—"

"If you're telling me a lie, I have every right to expose it for what it is," he said angrily.

She sank against the back of the couch and rubbed her eyes with her knuckles. "I'm not lying," she demurred. "That is, not really. Maybe just a little, but—"

"Then let's try to separate the truth from the untruth," he said softly. "Did you quit or did Ethan let you go?"

She knew she'd never get away with any more untruths. "Ethan let me go."

"Why?"

She took her hands away from her eyes and looked at him. "You'll have to ask him that, Nate, but I hope you won't. He's entitled to some privacy."

Nate was silent for a moment, then spoke again. "Okay, you're right. It doesn't take a rocket scientist to figure that one out, anyway. Living in the same house with a beautiful young woman has got to be a temptation for a bachelor Ethan's age. I'm proud of him for behaving like an adult and not giving in to that temptation."

"Then you won't put up a fuss about him sending me away again?" she asked.

He shook his head. "No. I won't make things even more difficult for the two of you. I'd have understood the first time he sent you away if he had come to me and told me what was going on. It was being left in the dark with no explanation that upset me so."

He sighed. "So, when are you leaving?"

"As soon as my agency has a new assignment for me," she said. "Probably in a week or so, but I don't know what Ethan is going to do about you and Danny. He said something about canceling his summer school classes and using the time to find permanent help."

She stood up and stretched. "Meanwhile, today is Sunday and there are lots of want ads in the paper. I'm going to go through them and look for a place to live."

* * *

Finding a rental that suited Brittany's qualifications wasn't as easy as she'd expected. A lot of them were in the wrong parts of town. She was going to live alone, and she wanted to feel safe.

Others were sublets, apartments or rooms available on a temporary basis by out-of-town students who would be coming back to them when school started again in the fall. Brittany didn't want to have to move twice. Once was quite enough.

The few that really suited her were too expensive. She could never afford them on her salary.

Meanwhile, the days went by and she continued to take care of Nate and Danny while Ethan worked, and their financial arrangement remained the same.

What puzzled her most was the fact that he seemed perfectly content to have her there. Why? If her presence disconcerted him when she was working for him, why wasn't it even stronger when she was living with them?

The tension between them was still just as strong, but he seemed to have it under better control than formerly. Did that mean he was learning to live with it? If so, it wasn't very flattering. Every Beauty wanted a Beast who would grieve for her after she was gone.

Rubbish! This was no fairy tale and it was time she got on with her life. She was going to stop being so picky and rent the first available quarters she could afford.

At the end of the week, Saturday morning to be exact, the phone rang while they were all having breakfast in the room off the kitchen, and since Brittany was closest she answered it.

"Who is this?" a female voice asked suspiciously from the other end of the line.

The voice sounded familiar but Brittany couldn't place it

immediately. Besides, she never identified herself or gave her address to strangers on the phone.

"Whom are you calling?" she asked.

"I want to speak with Professor Ethan Thorpe," the voice directed, sending cold shivers down Brittany's spine. She recognized it now. It was Ethan's ex-wife, Hannah Thorpe!

What did she want, and where was she calling from? Not that it was any of Brittany's business, but it froze her, nevertheless. Wordlessly she handed the phone to Ethan.

He looked at her questioningly then said, "Ethan Thorpe speaking."

Brittany saw the look of surprise on his face when he spoke again. "Hannah. Where are you?"

He was silent for a minute. "You're here? In Lexington? But I thought—"

Brittany shivered. What could Ethan's ex-wife, Danny's mother, want? It had been less than two months since she'd literally brushed the dirt of Lexington off her feet and left town, abandoning her little boy and all excited about her "fabulous" promotion.

Now she was back. Why?

"Danny's fine," Ethan said, apparently in answer to a question. Then he frowned. "You want to see him? Well, yes, I suppose it can be arranged. You're entitled, but I would have appreciated more notice. How long are you going to be in town?"

Hannah must not have answered directly because he looked puzzled. "What do you mean you don't know?" he asked. "I understood you to say you'd be traveling all over the world—"

She must have interrupted, because after a few moments of silence Ethan grumbled, "All right, I'll see you in an hour or so," and turned the phone off.

He handed it back to Brittany, then glanced around the table. "That was Hannah," he said unnecessarily. "She's in town and wants to see Danny."

Brittany wanted nothing more to do with that woman and she pushed back her chair and stood. "In that case you'll get along just fine without me. I'm going apartment-hunting."

Nate struggled to his feet, too. "Do you mind if I go along? I promise not to be a bother."

"Of course you can come," she agreed. "I'll be happy for the company."

"Hey, you guys," Ethan complained. "You're not going to leave me alone with her, are you?"

"Damn straight we are," Nate said as he cupped his hand on Brittany's bent elbow. "It'll give me a chance to take my best girl to lunch."

"Look, I'm serious," Ethan insisted as he, too, stood. "Dad, you know Hannah and I can't get along together for any length of time before the sparks start flying, and I don't mean romantic ones. At least if you and Brittany are here it might keep things a little more civilized."

Nate snickered. "If Hannah comes here and finds Brittany living with you and taking care of her son, there's going to be all hell to pay and you know it!"

Ethan's face went pale and he sat back down. "Oh, damn, I forgot about that!" he moaned.

"Well, you'd better start thinking about it," Nate advised, "because she's one jealous woman. She may not want you, but neither will she let any other gal have you. I suggest you let Brittany and me get out of here before she arrives."

Ethan nodded. "You're right. I don't want either of you exposed to her rotten moods."

He got up again and washed Danny's face and hands clean of oatmeal and mashed fruit while Brittany and Nate scattered to their rooms to make themselves presentable.

She applied makeup, brushed her hair and was ready within a few minutes, but Nate was slower. He shaved, changed his clothes and needed extra time to tie his dress shoes and button his shirt buttons. Ethan and Brittany fidgeted downstairs, but neither was willing to rush him.

Finally he was ready and they were all standing in the foyer while Brittany rummaged in her purse for the car keys when the doorbell rang. Brittany's heart nearly stopped beating, but Ethan glanced at his watch.

"Don't worry," he told Brittany when he saw her wince. "It's only been half an hour since I talked to Hannah. She said it would be at least an hour before she got here.

He walked over and opened the door. There, standing on the porch, was Hannah! Even though Brittany had seen Ethan's ex-wife only once, the image of her was branded in her memory. At that time Hannah had been in the middle of packing to leave town and was dressed in jeans and a shirt.

Today she was wearing a gray silk designer pantsuit trimmed with pearl buttons, and matching spike-heeled sandals. Her makeup was expertly applied and she wore perfume from one of the finest cosmetic houses in Europe.

No, there was no overlooking Hannah Thorpe! Dressed up or down, she was unforgettable.

"Sorry if I've inconvenienced you by arriving early," she said breezily as she walked past Ethan and into the foyer, "but I have a lot to do today. Ah, there's my baby," she said, and held her arms out to take Danny from Ethan, who was holding him.

Danny shrank back and hid his face in Ethan's neck.

Hannah gave Ethan a dirty look and tried again. "Danny, it's Mommy. Come here and give me a hug."

She put her hands on the child, apparently intent on pulling him away from Ethan, but Danny shook them off. "No! Daddy! Daddy!"

Ethan patted Danny's back and tried to calm him, but he wouldn't raise his head or look at Hannah.

She scowled. "What's the matter with him? I always told you you spoil him."

"You're scaring him," Ethan said tersely. "If you'd lower your voice and stop being so aggressive he'd eventually make up with you."

"What do you mean 'scaring him'?" she demanded. "I'm his mother, for heaven's sake."

"A mother he hasn't seen for a few months," Ethan pointed out. "Give the poor kid a chance."

Hannah grimaced. "I don't have time to cater to his temper tantrums. We've got to pack his things. I'm on my way to Rome."

"Rome, New York?" he asked.

She rolled her eyes. "Rome, Italy. I'm getting married next month and we're going to live in Italy."

Ethan, Nate and Brittany—all three—sucked in their breath and chorused, "Married?"

Hannah looked annoyed. "Yes, married. Why does that surprise you so? Italian men are a lot better husband material than American ones. Antonio gives me everything I want."

"He must be a millionaire," Ethan muttered under his breath, but Brittany was close enough to hear and stifled a giggle.

Nate was the one who recovered first. "We're very happy for you, Hannah. Why don't we go down to the family room and you can tell us all about it."

Brittany didn't want to get caught up in that grouping and spoke up. "If you'll excuse me I'll be running along—"

Hannah glared at her as if she hadn't noticed her before. "And who are you?" Her tone indicated that she expected an answer, and it better be a good one.

Before Brittany could do so, Ethan jumped in. "This is Brittany Baldwin, Dad's nurse. You met her last time you were here."

Hannah's glance ran over Brittany's slender bare legs, small waist and firm breasts as if she were inspecting a side of beef. "Yes, I did, but I didn't expect her to still be here. What's wrong with you now, Nate?"

"Same thing that's always been wrong with me," Nate answered. "Diabetes, but now it's complicated with a touch of senility."

Hannah shook her head. "That doesn't sound like something you'd need a full-time nurse for. What's going on here? I never saw a nurse dressed like that before." She indicated Brittany's red shorts and red-and-white-striped shirt. "Aren't they supposed to wear white uniforms?"

She was talking about Brittany as if Brittany weren't even there, which riled her considerably, but before she could protest Ethan intervened. "Brittany's apparel is none of your business. Now, do you want some time with our son or don't you? I'm not going to leave him alone with you as long as he's afraid of you."

"Don't be absurd," Hannah said indignantly as she again reached for Danny, who was still clinging to his father. "I'm his mother! He's not afraid of me!"

Danny's little arms tightened around Ethan's neck and he wailed, "Daddy! Daddy!"

Ethan glared at his ex-wife and patted his son's back as he murmured, "Don't cry, baby. It's all right. Daddy's here."

Brittany was furious, but she didn't dare interfere. If she did that would make Hannah even more unreasonable. How could any mother be so self-centered that she couldn't see she was terrifying her own child?

It was Nate who finally broke the impasse. He took Danny from Ethan and, looking from Ethan to Hannah, said, "You two can stand here and argue all day if you want to, but Brittany and I are going to take Danny to the family room. We're missin' some of our best TV programs."

"Oh, but—" Brittany said, but stopped when Nate took her

arm and pressed gently on it, the classic sign to be quiet and follow his lead.

Brittany did, and she and Nate walked down the hall with Ethan and Hannah following behind them.

In the family room Brittany and Nate settled on the sofa side by side with Danny on Nate's lap, and Ethan and Hannah sat in separate upholstered chairs.

"I don't see why that child is being so obstinate," Hannah grumbled. "He can't have forgotten me. I haven't been gone that long."

"It's not that he doesn't know you," Ethan tried to explain. "It's your tone of voice and your general demeanor toward him."

"Well, he'd better get used to it," Hannah warned, "because he's going to be seeing a lot of me from now on."

A chill swept over Brittany and she huddled into the soft sofa as if seeking comfort. A glance at Ethan assured her that he was equally upset.

"What do you mean?" he demanded in a raspy tone. "You said you were going to get married and live in Italy."

Hannah tipped up her head and looked straight at him. "That's right, I am. And I'm going to take Danny with me."

Brittany watched as Ethan's face turned red and he rose to his feet. "Like hell you are," he thundered.

Chapter Ten

Brittany was too shocked to do anything but stare at the two antagonists locked in verbal combat.

"Just try and stop me!" Hannah seethed. "I'll take you to court, and don't forget, I'm his mother and the mother is always favored in a custody battle."

"Don't kid yourself," Ethan warned. "That may have been true years ago but not anymore. When we were first divorced we worked out a custody agreement for Danny that we could both live with. However, if the parents slug it out in court, the father and mother of the child are given equal consideration these days."

He paused and took a deep breath. "Also, when you decided to move to Chicago, you gave me full custody of Danny. So you can't take my son out of the country without my consent. I'll fight you through every court in the land!"

That stopped Hannah for a moment, but only a moment. "I don't believe you, but even if it's true, court battles are expensive and I'm the one with the money. Antonio has lots of it and he's very generous."

By now Danny was screaming in Nate's arms, and Nate was still sitting on the sofa, but he had a vacant, closed-off expression that worried Brittany. Ethan and Hannah were too engrossed in the conflict they were raging to notice anybody else.

A surge of fury replaced Brittany's shock. She'd had enough of this! She wasn't going to stay here and expose these two vulnerable people to this battle of wills.

She stood and took Danny from Nate. The child came to her willingly but continued to cry and hide his face in her neck.

She kissed the little boy's moist cheek and head and murmured reassuringly to him as she settled him on her hip and held out her hand to Nate. "Come on, Nate. Let's get out of here."

He put his hand in hers and stood, then walked hand in hand with her as they headed for the doorway and the hall beyond. Her intention was to get in the car and take her two charges someplace where it was quiet and peaceful, but she'd barely started up the hall when Ethan called to her.

"Brittany, where are you going?"

"Somewhere away from here," she answered over her shoulder. "You two have managed to traumatize both Nate and Danny. I suggest you have your differences resolved by the time we come back."

"You're not taking my child anywhere. I'm calling my lawyer," Hannah blustered.

Brittany ignored her and headed on toward the front door with Ethan right behind her. "Honey, I'm sorry," he said grimly. "I had no idea Hannah was going to pull something like this, but I can't let her take my son away from me."

"Of course you can't," Brittany agreed, "but my concern is for Nate and Danny right now. They're both getting much too upset by all the commotion—"

"I'm concerned about them, too," Ethan interrupted, "and

I don't like the way Dad looks. I know you're the medical expert here, but may I suggest that you take him and Danny upstairs, get Dad to lie down in his room and turn on the television. That will keep both of them distracted while Hannah's still here, and I'll get rid of her as soon as I can. Okay?''

Brittany stopped and turned to Ethan. In the last half hour he'd aged several years. His face was gray and lined with worry, and the shock that looked out of his usually placid brown eyes was mixed with anxiety and pain.

Her heart ached for him and she had a much better understanding now of why he shied away from another marriage, but apparently he'd been handling this woman's temper outbursts for years. He could take care of himself. Brittany's first duty was to her charges.

"Only if you promise to keep her away from both Nate and Danny," Brittany said. "I don't care if Hannah is Danny's mother, I won't have the poor child upset like this."

She didn't have to explain what "this" was. Danny was crying so loudly that she could hardly hear herself speak. His chubby little body shook, and he clung to her so tightly that she could barely breathe.

"Don't worry," Ethan assured her. "She's not going to get above the first floor."

He leaned forward and kissed Danny on the cheek, then put his arms around Brittany's waist, baby and all. "My sweet angel," he murmured. "I knew I could count on you."

With one hand he tipped her head up and kissed her square on the mouth, sending prickles of fire throughout her already-sensitized nervous system.

By the time Brittany got Danny calmed down and Nate tested and medicated, Ethan and Hannah seemed to be finishing up their quarrel. At least the second floor of the house was quiet, which meant they weren't yelling at each other anymore.

As noontime drew near, Brittany wondered how she could

go downstairs and fix lunch for Danny and Nate without drawing attention to herself. She didn't know for sure if Ethan had told Hannah yet about just what her duties at the Thorpe home encompassed, but she doubted it. They'd been too wrapped up in the threatened custody fight to think of anything else. Still, if Hannah was as jealous as Nate had implied, it wouldn't take much to set her off.

Danny would be happy with some of the snack food Brittany usually kept stored in her dresser drawer, but Nate was on a special diet and needed to eat at regular times. She had about decided to try sneaking downstairs without being seen when she heard angry voices floating up from the open foyer.

"You'll be hearing from my lawyer," Hannah said in a threatening tone.

"Don't bother sending him to me," Ethan answered furiously. "I won't talk to him. Have him get in touch with my lawyer."

"Oh—" Hannah hurled an unladylike epithet and immediately Brittany heard the big heavy front door slam shut.

Brittany's relief was palpable as she left Nate watching television in his room and took Danny with her downstairs to the kitchen. The library door was open and she could hear Ethan's voice talking to someone on the phone from inside.

Not wanting to eavesdrop, she put Danny in the family room with some of his toys and started preparing lunch. It was only a few minutes before Ethan joined her. The strain of the past few hours was plainly visible on his whole countenance and not just his face. His shoulders were slumped, his hair was rumpled, and he walked with a slightly shuffling gate.

Instinctively she held out her arms. He walked into them and wrapped her in a warm and tender embrace. They stood there for quite some time just holding each other until Brittany spoke. Her tone was filled with understanding and regret. "I...I can see now why you're so adamant about not getting married again, but not all women are such...uh, witches."

He rubbed his cheek against her hair. "Watch your language, my darling," he said lightly. "After all, she is my son's mother."

"Some mother," Brittany muttered. "Were you able to agree on anything?"

He shook his head. "Not a single thing. That was my lawyer I was talking to on the phone just now. I have an appointment to see him tomorrow morning. He handled our divorce and also renegotiated the custody settlement just recently when Hannah gave Danny up. He doesn't think she has much of a case, but—"

Ethan's voice broke and he clasped Brittany even closer, uniting their bodies in an erotic embrace. He was fully aroused, and she trembled as hot blood raced through her veins. "Oh, Brittany," he moaned. "Do you have any idea how much I want you? Need you?"

There was no way she could not know of his physical needs. Not with their bodies pressed so intimately together, and she was as hungry for him as he was for her. But there was one desire he'd left out. He'd said "I want you and I need you," but conveniently left out "I love you."

He was in a vulnerable state right now. Was she foolish not to press her advantage? She'd had this struggle with temptation where he was concerned before. She could submit to his ardor when Nate and Danny were down for their naps. It would be easy for her to take advantage of Ethan's need for her, and afterward he'd marry her. She'd never doubted that, but were "need" and "want" strong enough to build a marriage on? Or would he feel trapped and eventually compare her actions to Hannah's deceitful ways?

She stirred in his embrace and murmured softly, "Can we have this conversation later? It's past time for Nate to eat."

Just then Danny came scampering into the kitchen and attached himself to his daddy's leg. "Cookies," he said. "Want cookies."

Ethan kissed Brittany, then reluctantly released her and picked up his son. "I guess we're outnumbered by hungry family," he said with a chuckle, "but promise we'll take up where we left off later."

"Oh, we'll definitely do that," she agreed with a smile.

During lunch Nate asked Ethan if he and Hannah had come to a decision about Danny.

"The only thing we agreed on was to disagree," Ethan responded bitterly. "I have an appointment to get together with Zach tomorrow morning."

Apparently Zach was Ethan's lawyer, Brittany thought.

"Then we'll meet with Hannah and her attorney, Clifford Jensen," Ethan continued, "and we'll try to avoid a custody dispute. If she knows what's good for her she won't push too hard. Zach says the fact that she voluntarily gave up custody just a few weeks ago won't set too well with any judge."

"Even so," Nate persisted, "I heard Hannah say that going to court will cost a lot of money."

Ethan frowned. "Don't you worry about that, Dad. I can handle it."

Nate wasn't reassured. "You've got a lot of expenses, and now you've had to give up teaching this summer to look for somebody to take care of Danny and me. That's a good-size loss of income—"

"Dad, I told you," Ethan reiterated, "I can handle it. There's no need for you to worry."

"I'm not worried but I am realistic," Nate insisted. "I know what your salary is and I know how much lawyers charge these days. What I'm trying to tell you is if you run out of money I want you to sell the house."

Ethan gasped, then choked and dropped the fork he was holding as Nate continued. "It must be worth a lot considering its historical value and all, and we don't need such a big place.

At lease we don't need it as much as I need my little grand-son.''

Brittany glanced at Ethan and saw the way the muscles of his face contorted in his effort to hide the deep emotion his father's willing sacrifice was having on him. Picking up his napkin he held it to his mouth for a moment, then cleared his throat and put the napkin back in his lap.

"Dad, I appreciate your offer more than I can say," he said, "but there is no way I'd sell this house. Why, it's been in the family for generations!"

"It has, and I'm proud of it," Nate confirmed, "but Danny's only been with us less than two years and already he's worth a million times more to me than any house could ever be."

Nate looked straight at Ethan. "We do what we have to do, son, and eventually we have to make choices. I'm just saying that if during this custody thing you're ever forced to choose between the house or the baby, don't be too proud to level with me."

For once Nate was more lucid than Ethan. It was obvious he knew exactly what he wanted to say and how to say it. "After all, the house is your inheritance. Yours and Peter's. I'm just offering to turn it over to you while I'm still alive. Pete can invest his half, and you can use yours to pay legal fees."

Ethan was losing his battle with his runaway emotions. He took a handkerchief out of his pocket and blew his nose. "Dammit, Dad, I love you." he said brokenly, then pushed back his chair and hurried out of the room.

Once Ethan got himself under control and they'd finished lunch, it was midafternoon. Brittany put Danny down for his nap, and Nate went to his room ostensibly to read, but she knew he'd nap, too.

When she came back downstairs Ethan had finished loading the dishwasher and straightening up the kitchen.

"I hope we'll have a little peace and quiet around here for the rest of the day," she said with a sigh as she joined him in the breakfast room.

"If you're referring to Hannah's outburst, I can almost guarantee there will be no more today," he told her. "She and I will take that up again with our lawyers present tomorrow morning. Meanwhile I think you and I have some unfinished business." His voice was husky as he put his arm around her waist and led her to the library.

Brittany hadn't forgotten for a minute the "unfinished business" he was talking about, but she hadn't been sure he'd refer to it again. Usually he avoided close contact with her, but he'd badly needed her comforting support earlier and had accepted it gratefully.

He was a strong man, though, and now he'd had a little time to recover from the shock Hannah's pronouncement had given him to start planning the best way to fight for his son. She was pretty sure those plans weren't going to include her. Nevertheless she relaxed and walked along beside him like a lamb to the slaughter.

But Brittany was no lamb! When she saw something she wanted she fought for it, and she wanted Ethan and the child who came with him.

She could make him happy. She knew she could, but only if he'd let her. She couldn't blame him for evading matrimony if what she'd seen today was a sampling of what he'd endured during his former marriage. But why should she, Danny and Nate, as well as Ethan, have to suffer for Hannah's nasty disposition?

Brittany was nothing like Hannah. Even Ethan had admitted that, but apparently he wasn't willing to trust any woman after his miserable existence with his ex-wife.

That wasn't fair. Not to him and not to Brittany. She knew

he didn't want to fall in love again, but she also knew he wanted her badly. Was there really that much difference in the two emotions? It seemed to her that "want" could easily become "love" if he'd just open up and admit it.

He shut the door and they settled down on the oversize sofa facing the fireplace. Ethan put his arms around her and cradled her close. "You're so soft and cuddly," he whispered in her ear. "It's all I can do to keep my hands off you."

That seemed like a strange thing to say considering that at the moment his hand was resting on her bare thigh below the cuff of her red shorts. "Have I ever indicated that I don't want you to touch me?"

He tugged gently at her earlobe with his teeth. "No, and that's what's driving me crazy."

"Then why don't you follow your natural instincts?" she asked softly. "Why do you let that harridan of an ex-wife of yours dictate the course of your life?"

She felt his muscles stiffen. "I don't—"

"Oh, yes you do," she insisted. "You're doing it right now. You're emotionally pushing me away even though I haven't done anything to you except love you."

He groaned and lightly kneaded her thigh. "I'm not pushing you away, sweetheart, even though I know I should be. Or maybe I am, but it's not just because of Hannah. It's the difference in our ages that makes a relationship between us impossible. You don't love me. It's just infatuation—"

"Don't tell me what I feel," she said, bristling, and tried to pull away from him.

He tightened his hold on her to keep her from escaping, but his voice was low and husky as he said, "You're right, I can't truly know how you feel just as you can't know how I feel, but neither can I take advantage of your loving nature just because I need you so much."

He gently positioned her head back to his shoulder and again she slumped against him, unable to stay mad. She knew he meant well and that he really believed the gap in their ages was an impenetrable barrier to their ability to be happy together.

She turned her head slightly and kissed the side of his throat. "I'm surprised Hannah would want to take Danny to Italy with her," Brittany said, changing the subject. "She didn't have any qualms about turning him over to you when she moved to Chicago. Why is she so eager to take him out of the country to live with her when she knows you will oppose it?"

Ethan's hand moved up an inch or so and the muscles in her leg jerked. "I asked her the same thing," he said, "and you're going to find this hard to believe, but she told me Antonio loves children and wants a big family—"

"But surely she can give him children of his own," Brittany interrupted.

He shook his head. "No, she can't. She didn't even want Danny, and after he was born she had minor surgery to make sure there would be no more babies. She's afraid to tell him the truth. He comes from one of those big loving Italian families and he'd never understand, so instead she told him she couldn't have more children because of 'complications' when Danny was born."

Brittany felt her eyes widen with dismay. "You mean she'd lie about a thing like that in order to get a man to marry her?"

His hand moved to caress her inner thigh and she squirmed with building excitement. She'd never before experienced such an erotic touch.

"Not only that," Ethan said, "but that's when he insisted she get custody of Danny again. He thinks Hannah should raise her own child and he also wants to adopt others. Apparently, he really is a nice guy who loves kids and wants to make life easier for those with no homes of their own. But my son has a family and I'll never let Hannah take him away from me."

Brittany was incensed. "I sure wouldn't want to bet on the longevity of that marriage."

He shook his head. "Neither would I, but in the meantime I don't want Danny subjected to the quarrels they're bound to have once Antonio gets to know his bride. I swear Hannah is never happier than when she's engaged in a blazing battle with somebody, and that's not just an unkind remark. It's the truth. I tried to get her to go for counseling. I even offered to go with her, but she'd have none of it."

She could tell he was getting upset. His heart speeded up and his breathing became labored. Tentatively she put her palm on his chest and rubbed it gently in an effort to calm him down. The muscles beneath his T-shirt flexed, and her own heart started thumping.

"You know, you're making it awfully difficult for me to concentrate on this conversation, don't you?" he said, and picked up her hand to kiss her palm before putting it back on his chest and holding it there.

"Sorry about that," she apologized, but made no effort to remove her hand. "I'll try to control myself."

With her tongue she played with his earlobe for a moment, then changed the subject. "About the custody suit, surely no court would allow a child to be taken away from his father and out of the country to live just because his mother needed an acceptable excuse for not having more children."

"Oh, I'm sure none would," he agreed, and pressed her closer against him, "but Hannah has no intention of testifying to her real motive in court, and she says if I try to get it admitted she'll deny everything."

Brittany couldn't believe what she was hearing. "You mean she'd commit perjury to get custody of a child she doesn't even want to be bothered with?"

Ethan shook his head sadly. "I don't know. In spite of her thorny disposition I've always found her to be basically honest. However, if snaring this millionaire is so important to her she might.

"It's not as if Danny wouldn't be well taken care of," he continued, "he would be. She'd make sure of it, but she wouldn't do it herself. She'd hire people to do it for her. He would never get the tender loving care from her that all children need, whereas I would give it in abundance."

Brittany looked up and licked the hollow beneath his ear. "Mmm, you taste good," she whispered as she pulled his shirt from beneath the waistband of his jeans and worked it up to his armpits. "Now, put up your arms," she commanded lovingly.

He did as he was told and she pulled the shirt over his head. "Young lady, are you hitting on me?" There was humor mixed with the frustration in his tone.

"Yes, sir, I am," she admitted. "Do you object?"

"Object!" he muttered, and put his arms around her again. "I love it. Just make sure you don't bite off more than you can chew, as the old saying goes. My resistance to you is almost nonexistent."

"Speaking of biting," she said. "I'm very talented at that. Would you like a sample?" She devoutly hoped she could follow through with that untried boast.

Before he could answer she nipped him on one shoulder and worked her way across his breastbone to the other one. He shivered and leaned back against the sofa, then lifted her up and laid her across his lap so that his face was just above hers. She turned slightly so they were chest to chest, her arms circling his neck. He lowered his head and his mouth found hers, tenderly but hot with passion.

"You could get into big trouble teasing me like this," he warned her when at last they broke the kiss.

"I'm not teasing," she insisted. "If you want me—"

"*If* I want you," he groaned. "I've wanted you ever since I first saw you, and what's more, you know it."

She laid her cheek against his shoulder. "If that's true, and I'm not saying it is, then why won't you take what I'm offering?"

"You know why," he said, and cupped the firm rise of her breast gently. "We're both totally wrong for each other. You need a young man who will play baseball with your kids and grow old with you, and I don't need a woman at all."

Brittany clenched her jaw and resolved to blot out some of that smug assurance he so proudly displayed.

"So you don't need a woman, huh?" she challenged. "Well, let's just see about that."

Before he could suspect what she had in mind, she tightened her arms around his neck and fastened her lips against his, forcing them open. Her tongue invaded his mouth and for a few seconds she was in control. Then without her knowing just how it happened, he flipped them over so that she was lying on her back on the wide sofa with him beside her and one leg draped across her lower body.

She could feel his arousal against her hip. It was hard and throbbing and she knew that the one thing she wanted most in all the world was for him to make love with her right here and now.

It no longer mattered whether or not he loved her. She didn't even care if he was especially fond of her. She knew she was tempting him beyond his ability to resist, but she couldn't help it. She was as caught up in this inferno as he was.

Shyly she reached her hand down between them and touched him intimately.

"Brittany, sweetheart, this is not right!" It was half moan and half sob as he bucked against her hand, but he made no effort to pull away from her, instead moving further on top of her.

Suddenly, without warning, there was a sharp cry from the

foyer followed by the crashing sound of a heavy body barreling down the stairs.

"Nate!"

"Dad!"

Brittany and Ethan cried out in unison as they sprang apart and tore up the hall to the staircase.

Nate lay crumpled on the tile floor at the bottom. Brittany ran to him while Ethan said, "I'll call 911," and rushed to the nearest phone.

Chapter Eleven

When the police arrived Nate was sitting up on the floor and insisting there was nothing wrong with him.

"I just slipped on that step about halfway down and lost my balance," he explained. "I'm not goin' to any hospital."

"You were unconscious for a couple of minutes and your speech is a little slurred," Brittany said crossly. "You're going to do whatever the paramedics say is best for you." His fall had frightened her badly, and now her relief that he didn't seem to be seriously injured was so great that she wasn't inclined to cater to his stubbornness.

He opened his mouth to speak but the ambulance siren announced the arrival of the paramedics. They examined him thoroughly and, like Brittany, found no broken bones, but the injury he had was to his head so they advised taking him to the hospital where he could be given more extensive tests.

Nate was having none of it. "You guys are just in cahoots with the hospital to get money from my insurance company—"

Brittany had had enough. "Nathan Thorpe, you be quiet and get your keister on that stretcher right now!" she ordered.

Nate's eyes widened and Brittany was equally shocked. What had gotten into her? She'd never talked to a patient that way before. Even the paramedics looked somewhat surprised. Ethan was the only one who seemed to be taking it in stride and he was actually grinning.

The tension built and then she noticed lines of humor twitching at the corners of Nate's mouth and a sparkle in his dark brown eyes.

He laughed. A full rolling sound of pure enjoyment. "Feisty little thing, aren't you. And just what are you gonna do if I don't plant my behind on that stretcher? Wrestle me?"

The apprehension was gone and she grinned. "I might, and don't think I couldn't put on a good show," she threatened, "but I'm more inclined to sic Ethan on you."

Nate chortled. "Oh, well, if you're gonna get ornery..." He spread his arms and looked up at the medics. "How about a little help, guys?"

Brittany had found that humor in the right place could alleviate a difficult situation. Now she'd been proved right again.

The EMTs strapped Nate on the stretcher and wheeled him out to the ambulance. Brittany walked along beside him as he grumbled about this trip being a waste of time and money.

She heard Ethan ask the driver which hospital they were taking Nate to and advised them that he'd follow in his car.

The ambulance left and Ethan and Brittany went back in the house. "I wish you could come with me," Ethan told her.

"I wish I could, too," she said, "but I have to stay here with Danny. Emergency rooms are no place for a child unless he's the patient. Please call as soon as they've examined him."

He nodded. "I will, and Brittany..."

He paused then continued. "I'm...I'm sorry about what happened earlier...."

Her stomach lurched and she was afraid she was going to be sick. She didn't want self-reproach from him. That meant they were all the way back to square one again.

Well, that's where they were going to stay. No more making a dunderhead of herself. It was no wonder he didn't want to get involved with her. Her actions today had just proved to both of them how truly immature she was.

"Please, don't apologize," she begged. "I can't talk about it now. Besides, I'm the one at fault."

She hated the idea that either one of them was "at fault" for enjoying the perfectly natural sensations they'd been caught up in, but obviously he didn't share her feelings. He didn't want to make a commitment to her and she was finally getting it through her head that he meant exactly what he said. That he was sexually attracted to but not in love with her.

She could see from his expression that he was going to argue that last point and hurried on. "You promised Nate you'd be right behind the ambulance, and I think I heard Danny stirring from his nap, so let's postpone this discussion until later."

She turned and headed for the staircase.

It turned out that there was a long wait before Nate could be seen by the emergency room physicians, an even longer wait while they did the necessary scans, and in the end they recommended that he be kept overnight for observation.

Ethan called Brittany several times to let her know what was going on, a nicety she greatly appreciated, but when he called the last time to tell her they were checking his dad in and Ethan would be home soon she took a quick shower and went to bed. She didn't want to talk to him face-to-face.

The next morning Danny woke up earlier than usual, which meant no more sleep for any of them. Brittany dressed herself, then Danny, while Ethan put his clothes on and then called the hospital for news of his dad.

The three of them met at the top of the staircase and Ethan took Danny from Brittany.

"Let me carry him," Ethan said. "He's too heavy for you

to tote up and down these steps, and we don't want another fall.''

"How's Nate?" she asked as they walked down the stairs.

"He slept well with no medication," Ethan reported, "and they're just waiting for the doctor to come and tell them if he's to be discharged."

They came to the bottom of the stairs and headed for the kitchen. "What time is your appointment with Hannah and the lawyers this morning?" she asked.

"Eight o'clock," he answered. "The attorneys had to work us in to their schedules, hence the early hour. I hope it won't inconvenience you."

"Not at all," she assured him, and plugged in the coffeepot that she'd set up the night before. "If they release Nate from the hospital, shall I pick him up if you're not here?"

He put Danny down and the child went toddling off full speed ahead. "I'd appreciate it if you would. You'll know how to take care of him once you get him home."

"Yes," she said, and ran out of conversation. There was nothing more to say on that subject, and she certainly didn't want to talk about the brouhaha yesterday when she'd disgraced herself.

The silence between them expanded until Ethan's nerves were about to snap. How could he have let things get so far out of hand as they had yesterday? Talk about immature! He'd behaved like a teenager with more testosterone than good sense.

If Nate hadn't fallen and distracted them he'd have taken Brittany right there on the couch. He'd been powerless to stop, and no thirty-six-year-old man should lose control that completely.

Now what? They didn't have any common ground to bridge this gap. They didn't have the same values and they didn't communicate on the same level. He'd always known any relationship between them would come to this. It was inevitable.

To his relief the grandfather clock struck seven-thirty and broke his contemplation. He almost welcomed the coming tussle with Hannah and her lawyer. At least it would take his mind off this struggle.

"I'd better get started," he said. "I don't want to be late after the attorneys were nice enough to accommodate us."

He chased Danny down in the family room, lifted him up and kissed his round little cheek, then put him down, called goodbye to Brittany and hurried out of the house.

Hannah's lawyer was Clifford Jensen, young, brilliant and sought-after. Also expensive, but apparently Hannah's fiancé could afford him. His office was in one of the new mirrored buildings near the courthouse.

Ethan parked his car in the attached parking building and walked to the elevator. He couldn't help contrasting this setup with that of his own lawyer's. Zachary Oliver was the one who'd negotiated the custody settlement for the Thorpes the first two times, but those had been uncontested.

He was a man in his early fifties, moderately successful, and his father was a friend of Nate's. His office was in one of the older office buildings that was slated to be torn down soon to make way for a new one. It looked seedy and out of date.

This meeting was being held at Jensen's office because that's where Jensen and Hannah had insisted it be held. They'd trampled all over Zach's preference to meet in his own office. His lack of influence didn't bode well and Ethan worried.

Was he making a mistake by relying on a family friend as a legal adviser instead of selecting a more high-powered and up-to-date one?

Ethan was a few minutes early, but even so Cliff Jensen was already there and waiting. The two men introduced themselves and Cliff offered Ethan a cup of coffee. He accepted it gratefully just as Zach walked in, followed a few minutes later by Hannah dressed like the consummate professional she was.

Everyone was served a beverage and then, true to form, Cliff took charge of the meeting. "As I understand it, Professor Thorpe, you've told my client you'll fight her petition to regain custody of her small son. Am I right?"

"Danny's *my* small son, too," Ethan corrected him, "and you're right, I won't allow her to take him out of the country."

"Can you tell me why? She is, after all, his mother."

"And I'm his father," Ethan countered. "Up until two months ago Hannah had physical custody and I had weekend visitation rights, but then she relinquished him to me completely so she could resettle in Chicago and be free to travel—"

"Now, just a minute!" Hannah interjected angrily. "I only left him with you temporarily because my job required that I travel extensively, but from now on I'll be based in Italy—"

"A foreign country where he doesn't even understand the language," Ethan growled, "whereas I'll be right here where I've always been. I can give him a much more stable environment—"

From then on the conference deteriorated into point-counterpoint until the attorneys stepped in and silenced them.

"You're both too upset to be rational," Zach said, "and we're getting nowhere. I see no way to settle this but to let a judge decide. Is that agreeable with you?" He looked from one to the other and they both nodded their heads.

"All right then," he continued, "I'll set up a hearing date."

He picked up the phone from the desk and punched in a number.

Ethan shifted nervously in his chair. He hadn't meant to lose his temper. He'd intended to be cool, calm and professional. To present the facts without showing any animosity toward the mother of his child. But when she started presenting innuendos and half truths he couldn't let her get away with it.

Fortunately the attorneys squashed their quarrel before he lost control completely and told the lawyers the truth about why Hannah wanted custody of Danny. That could have been disastrous! He had no proof other than her confession, and no one had heard that but him.

He'd have come off looking and sounding like a disgruntled ex-husband who would bad-mouth his ex-wife and say anything to win his suit. That would have done him more damage than good.

His ruminating was interrupted when Zach put down the phone and groaned. Obviously he didn't have good news for them.

"What's the matter?" Cliff asked.

"Well, it seems the calendar is booked up for weeks," Zach said, "and we only have two options. One, we can go to the end of the line and wait our turn, which is unacceptable to both litigants, or they can take advantage of a last-minute cancellation and opening for tomorrow afternoon—"

"But that's great!" Cliff said enthusiastically. "You told them we'd take it, didn't you?"

Zach hesitated. "As a matter of fact, I didn't. I need to talk to my client first. Is there somewhere we can go..."

Both Cliff and Hannah looked puzzled. "You can use this room," Cliff said, and stood. "Hannah and I will wait in the reception area."

He motioned to Hannah, who rose slowly and followed him out of the room.

Ethan was as surprised as Hannah and a little afraid that Zach had made a big mistake that could cost him his son.

"What's going on, Zach?" He tried to keep his voice steady. "There's no reason to prolong this. If there's time open tomorrow, both Hannah and I will be happy to use it."

Zach shook his head. "You don't understand, but Cliff certainly will. There's just one judge handling custody cases to-morrow and that's Rose Stewart.''

Ethan blinked. ''But what does the choice of judge have to do with anything?''

''The choice of judge is always important,'' Zach informed him, ''but in this case it's lethal. Rose Stewart hates men! I've never known her to give custody of a child to its father unless the mother was proved unfit!''

Nate had been released from the hospital midmorning, and Brittany was giving Danny and him their lunch when Ethan came home. He looked haggard, and she could tell things had gone badly before he said a word. Their gazes met and meshed, and she winced at the anguish she saw in his eyes.

Her first inclination was to go to him, hold him and let him hold her, but she steeled herself against it. No more of that. No matter what had happened today she was moving out of the Thorpe house. It was the only way she could survive with even a modicum of dignity intact.

Nate's voice was the first to break through the clatter of Danny's spoon being banged on his high-chair tray. ''How did everything go, son?''

''Hi, Dad, good to see you home,'' Ethan answered, then sat down and proceeded to tell them about the morning's events.

''Naturally I didn't want Rose Stewart for the judge, but Hannah was delighted at the prospect of having her,'' he con-cluded. ''We argued back and forth for quite a while, but I gave in when Zach pointed out that we could always appeal if the decision went in Hannah's favor. Apparently quite a few of Judge Stewart's opinions have been overturned lately.''

''But does that mean Hannah can take Danny back to Italy with her now?''

Ethan nodded. ''I'm afraid so, Dad. That is, *if* the decision goes against us. So far we're only speculating about that. We'll find out tomorrow.''

Brittany's heart ached for Ethan, and also for Danny. How could Hannah be so cold-blooded as to bounce her little son back and forth between his mother and father with every whim that tickled her fancy? The poor child would grow up never knowing just who he was or where he belonged.

And now she, Brittany, was going to make this chaos even messier for Ethan. She hadn't counted on a hearing date being set this quickly and had used her spare time this morning to pack up her things and find a place to stay temporarily. She was all set to move out now that Ethan was home.

What should she do? He'd need someone to look after Nate and Danny tomorrow while he was in court, but she needed to leave him, his house and his employment immediately! Whether or not she stayed and for how long was no longer an option for her. Like Danny, she was beginning to feel like a rubber ball tossed back and forth according to Ethan's mood swings until she had no identity of her own.

She finally made up her mind as she wiped Danny's face and hands. ''Ethan, have you had lunch?''

''No, I'm not hungry,'' he said.

''Then could we talk as soon as I get Danny down for his nap?'' she asked.

She had her back to him, so she couldn't tell what his reaction was, but he'd tried to apologize to her for the unfortunate episode between them yesterday a couple of times and she'd put him off.

''Of course—'' he said, but was interrupted by Nate.

''Let me put the little guy to bed,'' he said, and stood up. ''I'll read to him. It's been a long time since I've heard *Peter Rabbit.*''

''All right,'' Ethan agreed as he lifted the cleaned-up child out of the high chair. ''I'll carry him upstairs for you and you can take it from there.''

He looked at Brittany. "And I'll meet you in the library in a few minutes if that's okay with you."

She nodded. "Fine," she said, and watched as they headed for the staircase.

Brittany had the few lunch dishes stacked in the dishwasher and was drying her hands when Ethan joined her in the kitchen. "Dad insisted he could handle Danny by himself," he told her, "so I let him do it. I don't like to make him feel helpless. It's so depressing to be told you can't do something you've always done in the past."

She hung up the towel she was using. "You're a very wise man, Ethan. You really should have studied psychology and taken up counseling."

He smiled and looked pleased for the first time today. "I did. I minored in psychology, but my major was English and the literary field. It's a lot less stressful."

She chuckled. "Well, I can't argue with you about that," she admitted as they crossed the hall and entered the library.

Automatically Ethan took his usual place behind the desk and Brittany sat in the chair across from him. It made for a formal arrangement, but she was grateful for the desk between them.

If he touched her she'd break down and lose control, and there was no way she was going to let herself do that.

She hurried to be the first to speak. "Ethan, I want you to know that I'm going to resign my position with you and move out of your house starting right now."

She watched the blood drain from his face, but his voice was under control when he spoke. "But where will you go?"

She took a deep breath. "I've arranged to sublease an apartment from a student at the university who is going home for the summer but will come back when school starts up again."

"But you didn't want to take a temporary residence," he reminded her.

"No, I didn't," she admitted, "but I'm afraid my sights have been set too high. I was too comfortable here...."

"And you're not anymore?" he said sadly. It was more of a statement than a question.

She looked away from him. "No, I'm not, and neither are you. My behavior yesterday was unforgivable—"

Ethan cut in. "No, Brittany, it was my fault, not yours. I knew that if you stayed with us something like that would happen, but still I couldn't let you go. Has your medical agency placed you in a job yet?"

She nodded. "Yes. I talked to them this morning and I can start Monday. But what will you do about Nate and Danny tomorrow during the court hearing?"

"That won't be a problem. Zach says I'm to bring Danny to court with me." He tried for a smile that wasn't very successful. "Maybe if I have to restrain Danny and Hannah sees him in one of his tantrums she won't be so eager to reclaim him."

Brittany would like nothing better than to appear in court with Ethan and his family. To testify as to what a great father he was to his son, and son to his father, but she couldn't do that unless Ethan requested it. Obviously he wasn't going to do that and he was right.

The last thing he needed was to have it brought to the judge's attention that Ethan had a young and pretty woman living in the same house with him and acting as a mother to his and Hannah's impressionable child. Even though the only reason Brittany was there was because Hannah had abandoned Danny to his father when the youngster became too much of a burden to her.

"You will wait and say goodbye to Nate and Danny when they get up from their naps, won't you?" Ethan asked.

Brittany had hoped to avoid that and spare herself some of the pain of parting, but she'd come to the conclusion earlier that she couldn't just walk away. Some kind of closure was important. To her as well as to them.

"Yes, of course I will," she promised, and handed him a white card. "Also, I've written down my new address and phone number. Please let me know how this custody hearing turns out."

He took it and put it in his shirt pocket. "You'll be the first person I call."

There was an awkward pause, then Brittany slid her chair back and rose. Ethan rose, too, and for a moment they just stood there gazing at each other.

"Well, I guess this is goodbye, then," she said, her tone harsh with misery that she hoped he wouldn't notice. "I...I've enjoyed working for you, Ethan. Taking care of Nate and Danny. Thank you for letting me be a part of your household...."

She didn't offer him her hand. She knew she'd cry if he touched her.

Through the tears that misted her eyes she saw his features contort as he turned his face away from her. "Please, Brittany, don't. You've brought us peace beyond measure and pleasure beyond price. I wish you a full and happy life—"

His voice broke and Brittany turned and fled upstairs to the room that wasn't hers anymore. When she got herself under control again she started carrying her suitcases and boxes downstairs and putting them in her car. On the last trip Nate came out of his room and saw her.

"What are you doin', missy?" he asked her. "Here, let me help you."

She relinquished the smaller suitcase to him. Not that he wasn't strong enough to carry the larger one, but she was afraid he might lose his balance and fall again.

"Where are you goin'?" he queried when they reached the tile floor.

Brittany put her piece of luggage down and turned to him.

"I'm moving out, Nate. I've taken a new job and found an apartment—"

"You mean you're leavin' us." It was more an accusation than a question.

"Yes, I am," she admitted. "It's time for me to get on with my life. I'm becoming too attached to…to Danny. I want a husband and children of my own."

"Well hell," Nate drawled, and put his piece of luggage down, too, "you don't have to go somewhere else to find that. You're a fine-lookin' woman. Any man would be proud to have you as a wife. If I wasn't so damn old I'd marry you myself."

"And if you propose to me I just might take you up on it," she teased, and gave him a big hug.

He hugged her back. "Is there anything I can say to change your mind?" he murmured against her ear.

She blinked back unwelcome tears. "No. I'm sorry."

"I'm sorry, too," he admitted. "That son of mine is making a terrible mistake and I think he knows it. I just hope it doesn't destroy him somewhere along the road."

A noise at the top of the staircase distracted them. They stepped apart and looked up to see Ethan standing there looking down at them with Danny in his arms.

"What's going on?" he asked suspiciously, then paused. "Oh, I see. Brittany has told you that she's leaving us."

Nate glared at Ethan, then turned and disappeared down the hall.

Ethan carried Danny down the stairs and handed him to Brittany. She took him and nuzzled his fat little neck. "Goodbye, Danny boy," she said as he wiggled with delight. "Be a good boy for Mommy and Daddy, and try to remember me. I'm the nanny who loves you best in all the world…."

Her voice broke and she knew she had to get out of there. With a hurried kiss on his cheek she handed him over to his father. "Goodbye, Ethan," she said quickly, then picked up her suitcases and left without a backward glance.

Chapter Twelve

When Brittany first woke up the following morning she was disoriented. The sun streamed through the window above her bed, so why hadn't Danny wakened her? He was always up at the crack of dawn and ready to play.

She blinked and held her arm above her face so she could see her watch. It was nine o'clock! That brought her to a sitting position and ready to spring out of bed when she remembered. She was miles across town from the Thorpe residence and Danny wasn't her charge anymore.

She dropped back down and rolled on to her side. That's why she'd slept so soundly and so long. She'd tossed and turned most of the night. Every time she'd started to drop off she'd think she heard Danny cry or call to her, and she'd wake up again.

Apparently the last time that happened her befuddled mind had finally accepted the fact that it was all right for her to sleep, and then she'd overslept.

So what was she going to do to pass the time until she started work on Monday? Four days with nothing to do and nowhere to go. How ironic that Ethan needed assistance with Nate and Danny so badly and she had more free time than she could fill, but neither of them could ask for help from the other.

Brittany spent what was left of the morning putting away her clothes and trying to make the grubby little one-room apartment more homey. Since she had no groceries she drove to the inexpensive chain restaurant a few blocks down the street with the intention of having lunch there and then going shopping.

It had sounded like a good idea, but the café was too warm and humid, the food unappetizing, and her mind kept drifting to later this afternoon when Ethan would battle Hannah for custody of their son.

It would devastate Ethan if he lost, and God only knew what it would do to Danny if he were left to the cold indifference of his mother.

The big clock on the wall told her it was ten minutes after one. Ethan had said their appointment with the judge was for two. What was he going to do with Danny, who was approaching the "terrible twos" and could turn into a squirming, screaming little hellion and interrupt the whole proceedings if restrained for more than a few minutes.

And Nate? What about him? He would probably sit quietly in the courtroom and take an active interest in the proceedings, but what if his mind wandered and he got lost again when Ethan was distracted? Ethan needed help in looking after his family while he was in court. He couldn't do it all by himself.

A wave of guilt swept over Brittany. What was the matter with her, anyway? Why was she sitting here worrying about the situation when she had the power to do something about it? If she hurried she could still get to the courthouse and volunteer her services to keep track of Nate and Danny during the proceedings. This custody thing was hard enough on Ethan without the added burden of trying to placate a rambunctious child and keep an eye on an elderly man with a penchant for wandering off.

She signaled the server for her bill and rushed out of the building. In her hurry to start her car she flooded the engine and had to wait. Then she hit almost every red light between the restaurant and the courthouse, so that by the time she arrived at her destination she was five minutes late.

Dejected, Brittany sat in the car with the motor running. Now what? Could she get into the courtroom without causing a disturbance?

Should she even try? Or would she do more harm than good by showing up? Would Ethan prefer that she stay the hell out of his family affairs?

With a sigh she turned off the switch. She might as well go in and see what was going on. She could stay out of sight if that seemed advisable or she could step in if Danny and Nate got unruly. Besides, she couldn't stay away. She had to be there. Had to know how things were going.

It didn't work out that way. Ethan and Nate were sitting on a bench in the hall outside one of the doors, and Nate was holding Danny on his lap. Ethan looked up and saw her, did a double take and stood to greet her, a relieved smile on his face. "Brittany! You did come after all."

He took both of her hands in his, and she wanted to fall into his arms, but that would be totally inappropriate. She wasn't going to make a fool of herself. "I thought you might need some help with Danny. Besides, I...I couldn't stay away."

He squeezed her hands. "I'm glad." His tone left no doubt that he meant it and she felt shaky all over.

She glanced at the almost-empty hall. "Haven't they called your case yet?"

Ethan shook his head. "The one just before us is running a little late. Hannah's not here yet, either."

Brittany had never been in court before, but it seemed that there was something wrong here. "Where's your lawyer?"

Ethan shrugged. "Zach was here but he left just before you came in to see if he could find Hannah and Cliff, her attorney."

It seemed to Brittany that things weren't very well organized for being a court of law, but before she could comment Danny called out "Mama, Mama" and held up his arms to her.

She took him from Nate and hugged him close even as she frowned. "I hope he doesn't call me that in front of Hannah. Would you like for me to take him home and look after him until you get there? I can take Nate, too."

"Not on your life, missy," Nate said. "I'm gonna stay right here."

"The judge wants Danny here," Ethan said, "but I'd appreciate it if you'd stay and help me keep him corralled. I'll deal with Hannah when and if it becomes necessary."

Before she could respond, the door across from them opened and several people came out of a small courtroom. A man in a uniform of black trousers and a white shirt approached them and said, "Your case is next, Mr. Thorpe. Is everybody here?"

Ethan opened his mouth, but before he could speak two other men came rushing down the hall toward them. "Sorry, but could we delay for a few minutes?" the younger and better dressed of the two asked. "I represent Ms. Thorpe, but she's not here yet. Must have gotten tied up in traffic."

"Well, I don't know," the bailiff said. "You'll have to talk to Judge Stewart, of course, but the calendar is pretty crowded."

He preceded them down the aisle. Nate and Brittany took seats at the back of the room while Ethan carried Danny and walked beside Zach up to the front. When the case had been called, Cliff asked for a brief stay since his client hadn't arrived as yet.

"Was she properly notified of the time and date of this hearing?" Judge Stewart, a no-nonsense woman, asked.

"Yes, Your Honor," Cliff said. "I talked to her last night to remind her just in case she'd misunderstood."

The judge looked down her nose at the attorney. "Then why isn't she here?"

Cliff winced. "I have no idea, but I'm sure she has a good excuse—"

"I'm not interested in excuses," the judge thundered. "I'll give her ten minutes to show up—" She banged her gavel and went into her chambers.

Ten minutes was barely enough time to change Danny's diaper before they returned to the hearing. Hannah was still nowhere to be seen in the courtroom or the hall outside it. The judge again banged her gavel and asked, "Has Ms. Thorpe been located?"

Cliff stood slowly. "No, Your Honor, she hasn't, but I'd like to request a postponement—"

Zach was on his feet. "I object! Ms. Thorpe had plenty of notice as to when and where this hearing was going to take place. She apparently didn't think that having custody of her child was important enough to interrupt her schedule—"

Out of the corner of her eye Brittany saw a second bailiff come into the room and walk silently down the aisle. He handed a sheet of paper, probably a fax, to Hannah's attorney and left.

The attorney scanned it, then seemed to read it again more slowly.

He looked at Zach then at the judge. "May we approach the bench, Your Honor?"

The judge nodded and the two lawyers stepped forward. Zach looked as perplexed as Brittany felt. Her nerves were about to explode! What could be important enough to interrupt court proceedings? Especially at this late stage.

Cliff reluctantly handed the paper up to the judge, who read it, her scowl getting blacker with every moment. When she finished she handed it to Zach, who also read it. The two men plus the judge looked stunned.

"Did either of you have prior knowledge of this?" the judge asked.

"No, ma'am!"

"Absolutely not!"

Zach handed the paper back to the judge, who took it and read aloud.

Cliff,
Sorry, but I'm not going to show up in court tomorrow. I'll be on a plane for Italy. My fiancé has changed his mind and doesn't want us to have Danny after all. That's okay with me. I never did want to be bothered with a small child, so tell Ethan he can have his son, and bill me for your fee at my address in Italy.

Hannah

Brittany couldn't believe what she was hearing. Hannah was withdrawing her suit for custody of Danny! But why had she started this in the first place if she didn't care enough for the child to see it through?

Nate pawed lightly at Brittany's arm. "What did she say, missy? I couldn't hear."

"Not now, Nate," she said. "I'll tell you later. I think the judge is going to speak again."

She was right. Judge Stewart looked at the men in front of her, then settled her gaze on Ethan. "Do you still want to petition for full-time custody of your son?"

"I most certainly do," he said emphatically.

She looked at Cliff. "Do you have anything to say, Mr. Jensen?"

It was obvious that Cliff was seething with anger at his missing client. "No, I don't, Your Honor."

"Then I hereby grant full and irrevocable custody of the child, Daniel Thorpe, to his father, Ethan Thorpe, until said child reaches the age of eighteen."

She banged her gavel with an air of finality and strode into her chambers.

When the judge was out of sight Ethan thanked the two lawyers, then rushed up the aisle to grab Nate and tell him they'd won. Nate was overjoyed. He picked Danny up and squeezed him while Ethan turned to Brittany and took her in his arms.

She knew they weren't being very dignified, but she was too happy to care. Instead, she threw her arms around his neck and felt tears of joy streaming down her cheeks.

"Oh, Ethan, I'm so happy for you," she said enthusiastically, "and what's more you won't ever again have to worry about Hannah trying to take Danny away from you."

"I'm happy, too," he said, and nuzzled her neck. "I'm so happy I want to celebrate. Will you go to dinner with me tonight? Just the two of us."

He was asking her for a real honest-to-goodness date, but that was not only inadvisable, it was impossible.

"But what about Danny and Nate?" she asked. "Who'll look after them?"

"That's all taken care of," he told her mysteriously. "My neighbor next door has agreed to come over and stay with them. She's an elderly widow and I don't like to impose on her, but she bailed me out a few times before you came along when I had something important going on at school."

Brittany was having trouble following his explanation. "You mean you set this all up in advance even though you didn't know whether or not you'd have anything to celebrate?''

He shook his head. "I knew that being alone with you tonight was vitally important to me whether I won custody or not."

Warning signals began popping off in her brain and she tried to force herself to heed them, but what the heck. She and Ethan were both entitled to celebrate this momentous occasion! What difference did it make when it was planned?

She stepped out of his embrace and walked along beside him out of the courtroom and down the hall.

"I—I'm pleased that you want to share your celebration with me," she stammered. "What shall I wear?"

He laughed. "A typical question. I've made reservations for seven o'clock at the Plantation House. It's semiformal, but as far as I'm concerned you can wear anything you want and you'll still be the most beautiful woman in the establishment."

It was a wonderful evening. Ethan arrived to pick Brittany up looking splendid in a navy-blue suit and white shirt with gold cuff links and a navy-blue silk tie. He even had a corsage for her, a delicate white orchid that he carefully pinned on her black chiffon dress.

She felt beautiful, and the look in Ethan's eyes told her she was.

The food and ambience at the Plantation House was excellent as always, and a small live orchestra played big-band music for dreamy dancing in the dimly lit room. Brittany made a determined effort to relax and enjoy herself, and not remember that this was the last time she and Ethan would go out together.

For the most part she was successful, but she felt a sharp pain in her heart when the music stopped and it was time to leave. They held hands in the car on the ride home and Brittany wondered what would happen when it came time to say goodbye.

They were listening to classical music on the radio, but the closer they came to her apartment the more stressed-out she felt. There was no longer any reason for them to stay in touch. She was sure he wouldn't call on her to baby-sit again, and even if he did she'd have to refuse.

Would she ever again love any man as much as she loved this one? He insisted she didn't know what love was, but she knew better. She'd always been in pretty good touch with her feelings, and she had no doubt that she loved Ethan deeply. It wasn't something she had to think about, it was an emotion she felt.

When the car slowed down she realized they were approaching her apartment. Sliding her hand from his, she reached for the handle on the door and turned slightly toward him. ''I had a wonderful time—'' she started to say, but he interrupted.

''May I come up for a while, Brittany? There's something I want to talk to you about.''

That was the last thing she'd expected him to say, and she was jarred right out of her ability to speak. Instead she sputtered, ''Well I... That is, what...''

What could he possibly want to say to her? They'd already covered all they had to talk about. Not once but several times. So often, in fact, that her nerves were rubbed raw on the subject.

''Please, Brittany,'' he pleaded. ''This is important to me.''

She took a deep breath to say no, but heard herself saying ''All right'' instead. Damn, she'd never been able to resist him!

She led the way up the stairs, then unlocked her door and stepped into the dark room to turn on the light. The room wasn't exactly in pristine condition. She was still getting settled and she hadn't expected company. Certainly not Ethan!

She'd met him at the door when he came to get her, and he'd pinned the orchid on her in the car.

He followed her inside and she wished she'd never agreed to this. It could cause nothing but pain for both of them.

"Would you like to sit down?" she asked, and waved toward the only upholstered chair. She didn't sound very welcoming, but then she hadn't intended to.

"Thank you," he said, but instead of taking the chair he walked across the room, sat on the edge of the bed and motioned her to take the chair.

"I...I had a wonderful time tonight," she started to say again.

"So did I," he murmured, "but that's not what I want to talk about.

Her eyes widened as he continued. "Brittany, did you mean it when you said you were in love with me?"

She gasped and felt the crimson tide of embarrassment color her creamy complexion. Was he mocking her? She'd never known him to be deliberately cruel.

"My feelings are no longer any of your business," she snapped, and stood up. "Now, if you'll just leave..."

She turned away from him, but he stayed sitting on the edge of the bed. For a moment there was silence. Then he spoke softly. "I love you, Brittany."

It was as if a bubble had exploded in her head. She couldn't believe what she'd heard. Why was he telling her he loved her when they both knew he didn't? Had he decided to seduce her, after all? Well, he was too late. She was no longer interested in an affair.

"No, you don't, Ethan," she said, her back still turned from him. "You want me, but that's no longer enough for me. I'm going to get married and have some babies."

She heard him get off the bed and come up behind her. He put his hands on her upper arms and pulled her back against him. "Good," he murmured, and rubbed his cheek against hers, "because I have something for you."

Her heart leaped at his touch, and she scolded herself for being so weak. This time she had to be strong.

She pulled away from his grasp and turned to face him. He looked as uncertain as she felt. "I don't want gifts from you, Ethan." She tried to sound decisive but it came out wistful instead.

"This isn't a gift," he told her as he took a black-and-silver gift-wrapped box from the pocket of his suit coat and handed it to her. "Please, unwrap it. You don't have to keep it if you don't want to."

Brittany knew that under no circumstances should she accept that package, but she also knew she was going to. Ethan had never given her a gift before and she couldn't resist opening it.

She took it from him and untied the silver bow, then removed the black wrapping paper. Underneath was a deep blue velvet music box.

"Oh, how beautiful," she exclaimed, and partially opened the lid that started the pure strains of "I Love You Truly" to fill the air.

She blinked back tears and wished he hadn't chosen that song, but it didn't matter. She couldn't keep it. "Thank you, Ethan, but I really can't—"

"You haven't looked inside yet," he told her. "Open the lid."

"Oh, yes, of course. I'm afraid I wasn't thinking." She opened the lid, and there inside the satin-lined box was nestled another, smaller velvet-covered one.

It looked like a jeweler's box, but surely Ethan wouldn't be giving her jewelry. A music box she might be able to accept, but jewelry— Never!

She withdrew her hand as though it had been burned.

"No!" It was a startled cry. "I can't accept expensive gifts from you. Do you really think so little of me—"

Suddenly, without warning, Ethan snatched the smaller box from where it lay inside the bigger one and held it out to her. "Open it, dammit," he growled, and put it in her hand.

Too startled to think, she put the music box on the lamp table and raised the lid on the small one. For a moment she couldn't believe what she was seeing. When her eyes finally adjusted she gasped with astonishment.

There inside was a pair of star-studded wedding rings. The most beautiful diamonds she'd ever seen. But why was he handing these to her?

She raised her eyes to find him hovering over her, a look of uncertainty in his expression. "They're magnificent, but why—"

His gaze fastened on hers. "I'm trying to ask you to marry me, sweetheart, but I'm not doing a very good job of it."

She blinked. Marry him! Why had he changed his mind about marriage? "But...but you don't love me."

He put his arms around her and held her tenderly. "I adore you. How could you possibly not know that?"

She was beginning to wonder if he'd lost his mind. "Well, for starters, because you keep sending me away. That sends a pretty strong message to the contrary."

He chuckled. "I can see where it might, but didn't you notice that I also kept bringing you back again?"

She shook her head. "That was only because you needed me—"

"I need you now," he interrupted.

"I don't mean that kind of need," she said, and tried to push away from him, but he held on to her.

"Sweetheart, I love you and need you in every way there is. I want you to marry me, live with me, have children with me. I want us to grow old together, although I'll be old long before you are...."

Quickly she put her hand across his mouth. "Don't say that," she said sternly. "We'll have many years together before we have to worry about that."

She saw the wide smile on his face and realized what she'd said. "Does that mean you accept my rather botched proposal?" he asked hopefully.

"Was there ever any doubt in your mind?" she whispered.

He drew her closer and lowered his head to her upraised face. "I love you, my darling," he murmured, and their lips met and clung.

*   *   *   *   *

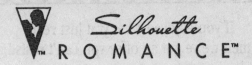

COMING NEXT MONTH

#1456 FALLING FOR GRACE—Stella Bagwell
An Older Man
The moment Jack Barrett saw his neighbor, he wanted to know everything about her. Soon he learned beautiful Grace Holliday was pregnant and alone…and too young for him. He also found out she needed protection—from *his* jaded heart....

#1457 THE BORROWED GROOM—Judy Christenberry
The Circle K Sisters
One thing held Melissa Kennedy from her dream of running a foster home—she was single. Luckily, her sexy ranch foreman, Rob Hanson, was willing to be her counterfeit fiancé, but could Melissa keep her borrowed groom…forever?

#1458 DENIM & DIAMOND—Moyra Tarling
Kyle Masters was shocked when old friend Piper Diamond asked him to marry her. He wasn't looking for a wife, yet how could he refuse when without him, she could lose custody of her unborn child? It also didn't hurt that she was a stunning beauty....

#1459 THE MONARCH'S SON—Valerie Parv
The Carramer Crown
One minute she'd washed ashore at the feet of a prince, the next, commoner Allie Carter found herself "companion" to Lorne de Marigny's son…and falling for the brooding monarch. He claimed his heart was off-limits, yet his kisses suggested something else!

#1460 JODIE'S MAIL-ORDER MAN—Julianna Morris
Bridal Fever!
Jodie Richards was sick of seeking Mr. Right, so she decided to marry her trustworthy pen pal. But when she went to meet him, she found his brother, Donovan Masters, in his place. And with one kiss, her plan for a passionless union was in danger....

#1461 LASSOED!—Martha Shields
Pose as a model for a cologne ad? That was the *last* job champion bull-rider Tucker Reeves wanted. That is, until a bull knocked him out…and Tucker woke up to lovely photographer Cassie Burch. Could she lasso this cowboy's hardened heart for good?

CMN0600

Look Who's Celebrating Our 20th Anniversary:

Celebrate
20
YEARS

"Happy 20th birthday, Silhouette. You made the writing dream of hundreds of women a reality. You enabled us to give [women] the stories [they] wanted to read and helped us teach [them] about the power of love."

—*New York Times* bestselling author
Debbie Macomber

"I wish you continued success, Silhouette Books.... Thank you for giving me a chance to do what I love best in all the world."

—International bestselling author
Diana Palmer

"A visit to Silhouette is a guaranteed happy ending, a chance to touch magic for a little while.... It refreshes and revitalizes and makes us feel better.... I hope Silhouette goes on forever."

—Award-winning bestselling author
Marie Ferrarella

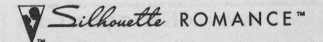

Silhouette ROMANCE™

ENTER FOR
A CHANCE TO WIN*

Silhouette's 20th Anniversary Contest

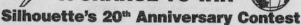

Tell Us Where in the World
You Would Like *Your* Love To Come Alive...
And We'll Send the Lucky Winner There!

Silhouette wants to take you wherever
your happy ending can come true.

Here's how to enter: Tell us, in 100 words or less,
where you want to go to make your love come alive!

In addition to the grand prize, there will be 200
runner-up prizes, collector's-edition book sets
autographed by one of the Silhouette anniversary
authors: **Nora Roberts, Diana Palmer,
Linda Howard** or **Annette Broadrick**.

DON'T MISS YOUR CHANCE TO WIN!
ENTER NOW! No Purchase Necessary

Silhouette®

Where love comes alive™

Visit Silhouette at www.eHarlequin.com to enter, starting this summer.

Name: _____

Address: _____

City: _____ State/Province: _____

Zip/Postal Code: _____

Mail to Harlequin Books: **In the U.S.:** P.O. Box 9069, Buffalo, NY
14269-9069; **In Canada:** P.O. Box 637, Fort Erie, Ontario, L4A 5X3

*No purchase necessary—for contest details send a self-addressed stamped envelope to:
Silhouette's 20th Anniversary Contest, P.O. Box 9069, Buffalo, NY, 14269-9069 (include
contest name on self-addressed envelope). Residents of Washington and Vermont may
omit postage. Open to Cdn. (excluding Quebec) and U.S. residents who are 18 or over.
Void where prohibited. Contest ends August 31, 2000.   PS20CON_R2